The Red King

The Tarot Legacies
Book 3

Victoria Belue

This book is dedicated to my great-aunt,
Edna Gertrude Beasley.
She was a fearless trailblazer at the beginning of the twentieth
century who fought for women's rights, traveled the world, and
wrote a stunning, unapologetic autobiography, My First Thirty
Years, originally published in 1925, that was not only banned in
the United States and the United Kingdom, but most copies were
burned.
She had the same Paris, France publisher as Ernest Hemingway
and James Joyce, Robert McAlmon at Contact Editions, who
remarked that of all the authors whose books he published the
most temperamental "were both Gertrudes," referring to
Gertrude Stein and my great-aunt.
In 1989, legendary author Larry McMurtry republished a
limited edition of her book, calling it "one of the finest Texas
books of its era; in my view, the finest."
Gertrude, at the age of 35, was deported from London because of
her book and thrown into an asylum when she landed in New
York. She was held there for the remaining twenty-five years of
her life.
In letters, she mentioned other manuscripts that she had written
which were even more candid and explosive than her banned
book. These works were never published and have disappeared.
The fact that she ran the bookkeeping department at the asylum

provides evidence that she wasn't suffering from any mental disorder as was claimed but was instead confined due to her liberated behavior which today would be considered tame.

This sad and infuriating history of my great-aunt is only tempered by my thought that she would have enjoyed the tales of my strong-willed, independent character of Vesta Beauvais. This book is a salute to her spirit and the spirits of those like her.

Contents

Chapter One

The crescent moon hung low in the night sky like an overlooked ornament on a discarded Christmas tree. Vesta stared at it from her apartment window high above Manhattan until a cloud slid across the silver orb, obscuring it from view. She turned from the jagged skyline to finish dressing.

Six months had passed since she last heard from Liam. A lot had changed during that time, yet she still held the image of him at Villa Spada frozen in her mind, looking broken and sad. As well he should after calling the other trionfi members to join her mission to bust Valentina's drug smuggling ring. Especially after she forbade him from doing so. Everything turned out well in the end, but she felt the sting of his betrayal and he knew it.

His sudden call to meet for dinner caught her by surprise. She had truly missed him, and it would be good to see his smiling face again. Shoved to the back of her mind was the niggling awareness that there was problem, a shift in her ability and the reason for his call. Certain that her newly mastered InSight would catch anything out of place, especially regarding someone she loved, she allowed that assumption to be her first mistake.

Vesta picked up her new Alexander McQueen faux snake-skin dress off the sofa and slid into it. A sigh floated from her lips as she tried to pull up the zipper on the back.

"Sandor." She aimed her voice toward the bedroom. "Would you come help?"

"I'm right here."

"Oh." She twitched at his sudden touch as the zipper glided up.

"Impeccable timing is one of my gifts as the Magician of the trionfi, remember?"

"Yes, but you scare the crap out of me sometimes when you do that."

Vesta grabbed a pair of black Manolo Blahnik stilettos and sat down on the sofa to slip them on.

"You look gorgeous. Is that new?"

"From Alexander's spring collection."

"And you're the first girl on the block to have one." Sandor smiled. "Or did you use your High Priestess InSight to grab one early from Mr. McQueen?"

"I don't need to do that. We're friends."

Vesta stood up and turned to face him. The pupils of Sandor's eyes widened as he wrapped his arms around her waist.

"Can I have a few minutes to charm this snake?"

Vesta used a gentle motion to push his arms away even though he looked devastatingly handsome. His dark brown hair, vibrant blue eyes and chiseled jawline were set off by a perfectly tailored navy Ralph Lauren suit, crisp white shirt and the Armani tie she bought for him on their last trip to Venice.

"We have to go. Traffic will be horrendous in midtown."

Reservations at eight o'clock weren't easy to come by on

short notice at Le Bernardin on a Saturday night. But Vesta had become friends with chef Éric Ripert shortly after he arrived at the restaurant seven years earlier. She only called on him when the situation demanded. Besides, having the legendary rock star Liam Spencer in the restaurant never hurt business.

As they waited to be seated Vesta noticed her sister Amara and her partner Jared Schultz sitting at a large table in the center of the room with several other people.

"How many trionfi can you fit into a three-star Michelin establishment at once?" Vesta whispered to Sandor.

"More than you think," he said. "Sitting beside Amara, our Empress of the tarot, and her overly confident lover, otherwise known as the Emperor, is Javier Garcia, the King of Pentacles in our little club."

Vesta flicked her eyes at Sandor. "That guy is a tri-phony too?"

"He certainly is. And I'm fairly certain those are his two children with him. I haven't seen them since they were little kids, but the one with the white button-down shirt and short black hair is probably Luciana. And the other one with the curly dark hair and black nerd glasses would be Alejandro."

"They're all three part of the Pentacles family?"

"Yep."

"So, the son, who looks to be about fifteen, would be the Page of Pentacles. Is the daughter known as the Knight even though she's female?"

"Sure, women can be Knights and Pages."

"I just wanted to get their titles straight."

"Yeah, when the original paintings of us were made back in the Renaissance the keepers of our secret story represented the children of the royal families as male to emphasize their capability to carry out the jobs they were responsible for. Sexist, I know, but those were the times."

"And their strength is all about money, property, and material things like that?"

"Right again." He nodded his head. "I can tell you've been studying more than just your own gifts."

"Of course," she said.

"Yeah," Sandor said, eyeing the table. "Javier really took advantage of falling land prices in Spain a few years ago. Almost cornered the market in relieving heirs of their financially burdensome estates. At deep discounts. Very bright, but very slippery."

"Why are Amara and Jared dining with him?"

"I have no idea," Sandor said as he looked at her. "But let's find out." Vesta followed him as he made his way across the restaurant.

"Good evening," he said walking up to the table.

"Ah, good evening." Javier stood up. He cut a dashing image with his wavy dark hair, closely cropped black beard and mustache against tanned skin. His dark eyes matched the color of his Balenciaga suit. He shook Sandor's hand. "Good to see you, my friend," he said with a slight French accent. Turning to Vesta, he bowed slightly. "And you, your Highness, such a pleasure to see you again. I am Javier Garcia."

She put out her hand. "Please call me Vesta."

"Congratulations. I heard of your recent revelation."

Sandor laughed. "Yeah, she's back in the game at top form now."

"That's wonderful," Javier said. "Would you care to join us?"

"We have a table. I just wanted to say hello and introduce Vesta."

"Certainly. And, your Highness, let me introduce you to my family," Javier said. "This is my daughter Luciana." He nodded across the table.

The young woman with bright, dark eyes looked at Vesta and smiled. "Hi, call me Luc."

"And my son Alejandro."

As Vesta glanced next to Luc, she realized the young man wearing the nerdy glasses had been staring at her with a rigid, penetrating gaze. She recoiled a fraction of an inch but caught herself.

"How are you Alejandro?" she said with a cool voice.

"Fine," he said, continuing to stare at her without blinking.

Javier noticed Alejandro's rude gaze and let out a little nervous laugh. "And of course, you know Amara and Jared," he said trying to divert from his son. "You and Amara are the most beautiful women in the room tonight, no question."

Amara smiled politely, signaling her understanding of Javier's discomfort. But she did indeed look stunning with her shoulder-length blonde hair, bright blue eyes and perfect pale complexion. Dressed in a burnished gold Oscar de la Renta slip dress and a simple string of black cultured pearls—undoubtedly from Jared—she truly was the centerpiece of the room.

"Nice to see you both," Jared said smiling broadly with his own sky-blue eyes sparkling from his tanned face. His short blonde hair always looked like a slightly messy afterthought, even though she knew he worked to make it seem that way.

"Vesta, I was planning to call you next week about setting up a Sybarite fashion show for our upcoming luncheon for Conscious Evolution Partners," Amara said. "I was just discussing it with Javier. He has been enormously generous in underwriting the event."

"Sure. No problem."

The maître d' approached Sandor to tell him their table was ready.

Sandor nodded and looked back at the group. "Okay, well, good to see you all."

"A pleasure," Javier said.

"Yeah, Liam's in town and meeting us here," Sandor said. "Get ready for the paparazzi and flashbulbs outside when he arrives."

"Okay. We'll stop by to say hello on our way out," Amara said.

Vesta and Sandor walked toward a table in the far corner of the restaurant, away from the street-facing windows. The maître d' pulled out a chair for Vesta.

"Mr. Spencer has just arrived. I believe he's signing a few autographs, but I'll show him over when he's ready," the man said.

"Thank you," Sandor said as he sat down.

Leaning toward Vesta after the maître d' left, he slid his gaze toward Javier. "That guy always has something up his sleeve."

"I thought that was you," Vesta said, adjusting the napkin in her lap. "With something always up your sleeve."

Sandor smiled and pulled a fresh red rose from the inside pocket of his jacket and handed it to her. "Well, I do but I don't trust him."

"Why? Because he makes more money than you?" Vesta asked as she slipped the stem of the rose carefully through the button hole of Sandor's jacket lapel.

"I could make as much as he does if I wanted to." He adjusted the rose with a slight tweak. "I just don't feel like jacking people to do it."

"You're one of the top hedge fund managers in the world, of course you jack people."

"Not like he does."

"According to what you and Amara have told me, the four royal families of the tarot don't really retain their memories life after life like we in the major arcana do." Vesta raised her eyebrows. "Well, except for when we erase them with a spell."

"That's right."

"Why did Javier just say it was nice to see me again? He has to be referring to meeting me in a previous life. How did he remember that?"

"Yeah, that spell you put on yourself wiped out almost all of your memories of past lives even after it was broken. Your InSight is back, but those memories may be gone forever. You'll have to wait and see if they even come back in the next life."

Sandor leaned back in his chair. "As for Javier's memories, and those of the other royal families of the trionfi, they don't bring many memories with them life to life. Only the big stuff like births and deaths. But they have volumes of diaries—centuries old—that record people and events in each lifetime. Every time Javier reincarnates, he has an inkling of who he is as part of the trionfi but it's his family, his children, if they're still alive, or sometimes grandchildren, who give him the big update when he turns ten. He's expected to spend lots of time in the family library to get up to speed on details."

"Oh, that's right. I remember someone mentioning that when we were in Key West last October. But I thought the minor arcana royal families were created by the Elders for the purpose of protecting those of us in the major arcana, if we needed it."

"In the beginning, sure. But as the centuries dragged on, they lost a lot of their piousness and focused on exploiting their gifts. For our ol' buddy Javier over there, he has spent hundreds of years amassing a gigantic fortune in real estate, art, and cash."

Murmuring voices rose in the room like a wave crossing a shallow pool. All heads were turning as Liam Spencer followed the maître d' across the restaurant. Dressed in tight black jeans, a black jacket, and black shirt unbuttoned to the middle of his chest, Liam sauntered toward her. She always admired how he could remain not just calm but completely unaffected by all the eyes scanning him whenever he was in public.

Sandor stood up when he reached the table. "Good to see you, old man."

"You too. I've missed you."

Liam grabbed Sandor in a friendly hug, then shot a quick glance at Vesta and smiled. She blinked and returned the smile. He moved to her chair, bent low, and scooped her up in his arms.

"I've missed you the most," he said with a quick squeeze. He sat down at the table with his back to the room.

A waiter approached and asked if they would like something to drink. Liam ordered his usual Gilpin's as a martini, his British accent making the order sound all the more necessary. Sandor asked for Macallan 17-year-old scotch neat, and Vesta almost purred the words, "Wild Thing" to the waiter.

"No vodka martini? I'm beyond shocked." Liam pursed his lips.

Vesta smiled. "A Wild Thing is the most alchemical concoction of Brooklyn Gin, Dolin Dry Vermouth, and pickled ramp with a wild black pepper tincture. Made exclusively here. It's incredible."

"Hmmm. And what do you know of alchemy?" Liam asked, raising his eyebrows to their peak.

"What?"

"Alchemy. You just said your drink was an alchemical concoction."

"Oh, that was only an expression. I don't know anything about it. Some moldy medieval guys trying to turn lead into gold."

"There was Isaac Newton too. He wasn't moldy or medieval," Sandor said.

"Whatever. You get my point, the cocktail is fabulous," Vesta said.

"Yes, well, just to set the record straight, alchemists basically want what most of the rest of us want, to connect with God," Liam said.

"By making gold?" Vesta asked, shaking her head.

"Absolutely. Achieving that feat was merely a metaphor for attaining connection to the Divine."

"Yeah, that's stretching it," Sandor said.

"No, it's true," Liam said.

"So, what brings you to town? Has your tour wrapped?" Vesta asked.

"Not quite. We have a show in Paris next week, followed by Italy, and South America after that. Just a bit of a break in the meantime for the crew and bandmates to reconnect with family. That sort of thing."

Vesta smiled. Liam's presence made her feel reconnected to something deep within her. She had missed hearing his voice and looking at his mop of brown hair that seemed to have a mind of its own.

"And you wanted to come see us," Sandor said with a grin.

"Actually, he wanted to see me," she said. "You just got to tag along."

"It's true, old chap," Liam said and turned to Vesta. "I had something made for you." He paused as if he didn't know what to say next.

Vesta noticed that his voice made an almost imperceptible shift from its usual lightheartedness to a serious tone. She eyed him closely for a moment. "For me?"

From the pocket of his jacket he pulled out a thin rectangular black box and handed it to her.

"What is it?" she asked.

"It's not a bowling ball," Sandor said.

Vesta took the lid off and dipped her fingers inside. She lifted up a necklace of small oddly shaped stones connected by a gold chain, a silver crescent moon-shape dangled down from the center. It was quite possibly the ugliest necklace she had ever seen.

"I remembered how much you liked that lunar shape from your previous go-rounds here," Liam said with a hesitant smile. "It was on your old card from the Sforza days to signify your intuition, InSight, right?"

Vesta nodded. Even before she had reawakened to her life as the High Priestess, she had been drawn to the shape of the crescent moon. Stunning in its silver-white brilliance against the black sky, outlining what couldn't be seen yet, unless the observer paid careful attention, foretelling what was sure to come.

"I noticed the crescent moon tonight. It looked just like this," she said as she let the stones roll around between her fingers. "And yes, I do love the shape. But I don't recognize these stones."

"They're very old. A gift from a friend. They supposedly align with your chakras, or some sort of thing, the jasper, cornelian, agate, and lapis." Liam waved his hand toward the center of the room. "I'm sure Amara could tell you all about the chakra connection."

Vesta once again caught a note of caution in his voice.

"I had the moon added to the necklace to make it more personal for you." He paused, clearly waiting for her reaction.

"Oh," she said eyeing the haphazard collection of stones that, on closer inspection, looked like they had deep scratches embedded on them, the gold chain crudely made and pitted in places. "It's very unique."

"One of a kind for my one-of-a-kind girl."

Looking up from the necklace, Vesta could see the anxious

expression on Liam's face. He so wanted her to like it. She could tell the months of not speaking had been hard on him. They were stressful for her too. He had been her best, and only, friend since college sharing soul-rattling moments as well as outrageously raucous times. She wouldn't destroy that.

"I love it," she said.

The almost desperate look in his eyes melted into glinting sparks that began to dance in his light brown eyes. And the silly smile which she loved so much spread across his face.

"It doesn't go with the python dress you're wearing though, I must say." He reached for his cocktail.

"Well, you're right," Vesta said. "But I will find the perfect outfit for it tomorrow." She reached over and squeezed Liam's hand. "Thank you for this thoughtful gift."

"It's my peace offering to you. And it's something I hope you keep close to you at all times. Will you? It's our bond of trust rekindled, alright?"

Vesta looked at Liam for a long moment. It had been difficult for her to forgive him. Betrayal was almost as bad as murder in her view, but she understood he did it with the intention of trying to help her. For that reason, she forgave him after months of wrestling with angry, bitter feelings. But he was like family, real family, to her and she didn't want to lose him.

She nodded. "Yes. I will keep it close. All the time."

The waiter arrived with their drinks. When each had their own, Vesta raised her glass.

"I would like to make a toast." She looked at Sandor and then Liam. "I turned forty a couple of weeks ago, but it has only been within the last year that I was reborn to who I truly am. And I want to thank both of you for your help and love along the way, even though I didn't recognize it as such at times."

"To your health and happiness," Liam said.

"To you finally coming to your senses," Sandor said with a wink. Vesta gave him a side-eye glance and shared a half smile.

The trio sipped their drinks and picked up their menus.

"Speaking of you coming into your own," Liam said, with an uncharacteristic tone of gravity. "Are you getting any alerts from your InSight lately?"

Vesta put down her cocktail and studied his face. Something was wrong but Liam was dancing around actually telling her what it was.

"What do you know that you're not telling me?" Vesta's eyes widened their focus on Liam. "Valentina and Raz are still sitting in the maximum security Metropolitan Correctional Center right here in Manhattan. I know because I'm to be contacted if anything with their status changes. And their trials aren't for several months yet."

"It's not the Ritz for that First Blood or Rasputin," Sandor said.

"Oh, I know. I wasn't referring to them." Liam lowered his voice and locked eyes with Vesta. "Have you spoken to Peter lately?"

"Peter?" She froze in place. "No. Why?"

"You're probably not aware of this, but Peter and I are close. He's been a great source of inspiration for my songs and music over the years."

"I didn't know that."

"Me either," Sandor said.

"Our conversations are bloody awesome. He opens my mind to all sorts of new ideas during those crazy walks around his labyrinth. Anyway, about two weeks ago I stopped by Chartres when we were on our way back to London. He wasn't there. At the cathedral, I mean."

Liam set his drink down. "It was odd, so I inquired with the priests who know he's grandfathered to the place, so to speak.

They said he'd been gone for almost a month. Disappeared without telling anyone he was leaving or where he was going."

Liam gazed down at the medallion hanging from the leather cord around his neck. A centuries-old depiction of him as the Fool clad in a tunic and tights, a pole slung over his shoulder holding a pouch was enameled on it.

"It's very strange. In all our lives, since you built the labyrinth for him, I can't remember him ever leaving for this long," he said.

"Well, I remember the late seventeen-hundreds when he wasn't there very much," Sandor said.

"That was during the French revolution! None of us took holidays there during those times."

"I'm just saying."

"Vesta, is your High Priestess radar tuned in to him these days?" Liam asked, his eyes searching her face with a seriousness she had never witnessed from him before.

"I think my InSight is working extremely well right now. And I'm getting alerts, as you call them, about all sorts of things."

She nodded toward Amara. "I helped her last month by tracking down poachers who were ransacking one of her foundation's outposts in Kenya and one in the rainforest."

"And you clued in that woman you know from the Bronx so she didn't take the fall for that slimy land developer's deal," Sandor said.

"True, but I would have seen that coming without my InSight." Vesta refocused on Liam. "If Peter were in trouble, I would have seen it. We've been connected in that way since we first met."

"I understand, but I know you're quite busy with your fashion empire too."

"My position as CEO and Chairman of the Board at

Sybarite does not interfere with my duties for the trionfi. I'm quite capable at managing both." A twinge of irritation sprang up her spine at the suggestion she might not be up to the task.

"I know you're incredible at juggling the pair, I'm just worried about him."

Liam stared at her for a moment as if he wanted to say something else, but he looked away and caught the eye of their waiter. As they ordered more drinks, they noticed the King of Pentacles pick up his cell phone and leave his table. Sandor looked at Liam after the waiter left.

"I introduced Vesta to Javier Garcia before we sat down. Have you had any significant contact with him this time?"

Liam shook his head. "Not for many lives. The last time was when I started that whole troubadour craze in the Middle Ages in the south of France. I was living in the Aquitaine at the court of William the tenth. He sent me to perform for Javier at his castle in the neighboring Basque region. As I recall, he wanted to make me his indentured servant or something and hire me out to other kings and lords. I've steered clear of him since."

"Typical Javier," Sandor said.

"Indeed. I may seem clueless and utterly carefree at times, but I'm my own man, let's all remember that. However, I have gotten to know his daughter, Luc, very well this time."

"Oh, some hiatus humps happening while you're in town?"

"No, Sandor. She's gay," Liam said with a quick, dry response. "And she's a music producer who has a keen ear for some exquisite melodies. We're working on an album together. Something very different from my usual rock anthems. I'll be in the studio with her on Monday. You should stop by."

"Yeah, I've got a full day already stacked. The market is cuing up for some hard times. 1998 is proving to be a challenge, even for me."

"What about you, lovey? Would you like to join us? You know I always appreciate your thoughts."

"I have marathon meetings with our home goods designers throughout the day to prepare for a new launch, but I may be able to get away after that."

"That would be great. Now, back to Peter." Liam wrinkled his forehead. "I'm really worried about him."

"Now Liam," Vesta spoke in a calming tone. "Since the episode on Valentina's island, I've devoted myself to developing my InSight. In fact, I've become so adept at it that I've created shortcuts to tap into it on command." She nodded toward Sandor. "As I sat here listening to you two, I slipped into my private space and felt my third eye begin to spin. It got warm and tickled a little, but that was all. Nothing about Peter came into focus."

Liam chewed on his lower lip. "Nothing at all?" He gave the necklace box sitting on the table between them a few thoughtful taps. "Not even him sitting on the beach somewhere in that dreadful black turtleneck sweater?"

Vesta shook her head. "Nothing."

"And you don't think it's odd that he's been gone a month from Chartres?"

Vesta smiled at him with love and patience. "Look, I don't remember Peter except for the brief times I've been with him at the labyrinth in this life. But I can tell you that I care a lot about him too. And I can see why I designed the cathedral for him."

She placed her hand on top of his. "I'm connected to him. I have been since before I knew how to control my InSight. He would come to me in my dreams. If he were in trouble, I would know it."

Chapter Two

Electric Lady Studios on West Eighth Street in Greenwich Village became famous from the day it opened almost thirty years earlier. Purchased by Jimi Hendrix—and designed for his specific tastes—it had hosted some of the world's most famous recording artists. Liam idolized Hendrix, so it was no surprise to Vesta that he always rented that studio when in New York.

She arrived a few minutes after six o'clock on Monday evening and found Liam in studio A. It looked exactly the same as the last time she was there. The grand piano sat on top of a large Persian rug in the middle of a room that had a curved wall. A huge mural was painted across it which Vesta had always interpreted as scene of Alice in Wonderland if she were to take an alien space-craft on a joy ride in outer space past the rainbow rings of Saturn.

Underneath Alice, Liam sat on the floor next to a Marshall amplifier. His fingers were picking out a slow tune on his favorite Fender Stratocaster guitar he called Siouxsie.

"Hey, sorry I couldn't get here sooner. Busy day for me. We're rolling out our new summer tableware line," she said.

"No problem. I was just composing a little something as a tribute to Wendy O. Something I've been working on since I heard the news. Do you remember seeing her and the Plasmatics at CBGB?"

"Of course. It would be difficult to forget one of her performances."

"Yes, she was brilliantly brazen, wasn't she?" He set the guitar down and looked at her. The light of her merry fool still shone in his face, she noticed, but it was dimmer.

"Hey, look," she said pulling the necklace he gave her from underneath her Donna Karan cashmere sweater, laying it on top.

"Cool." He gave her a slight smile. "Come listen to what we've been working on."

Vesta had hoped that his somber mood had lifted and her light-hearted Liam would be back after a couple of days, but if anything, he was even more melancholy. He stood up and walked toward Luc, who was tucked behind an acoustic screen across the room. On top of a desk sat a computer and an electronic keyboard. Luc was leaning forward in a chair with her arms propped up on the desk. A pair of headphones covered each ear. Her eyes darted toward them as they approached. She pulled off her headphones and smiled.

"Luc," Liam said. "Do you remember meeting Vesta the other night?"

"Yeah, you mentioned she might be stopping by today." Luc stuck out her hand. "Good to see you again."

"Thanks." Vesta shook her hand. "I can't wait to hear what you've been working on."

"It's quite a bit different from what I've done in the past," Liam said. "Luc, would you mind playing some of the tracks for Vesta?"

"Sure. Let's go into the control room so I can do a little mixing while we're listening."

Luc stood up and stretched. Vesta noticed her tall, well-toned body underneath her white button-down shirt and jeans. She pushed her short black hair away from her face even though it immediately fell back into place nicely framing her large dark brown eyes and fair skin.

Vesta followed Liam and Luc toward a control room stuffed with mixing boards, reel-to-reel tape recorders, speakers and computer monitors.

"Have a seat," Luc said. "Our engineer Michael left for dinner, but he doesn't mind if I play with his toys a bit. I take good care of them."

Liam pulled out a chair for Vesta and himself. They all three sat down and drew close to the mixing board.

"Back in ninety-three I met Luc after a Fad Gadget show in London."

"Actually, he was going by his real name Frank Tovey by then," Luc said.

"Yes, right. Well, anyway, he introduces me to this kid. I mean, she looked like a kid five years ago."

"I was a kid. Twenty, I think, when I met you."

"But Frank is telling me how she's creating all this innovative music. And he was one to talk. He used to create his own instruments out of old toasters and odd bits," Liam said. Vesta could hear a lilt of enthusiasm enter his voice and see a spark flash in his eyes.

"Anyway," he continued. "She gave me a card which by some miracle I held onto and we connected a couple of years later at her parents flat in London. I heard her music, and it tripped a switch in my bloody head."

Luc smiled. "I had just begun experimenting with my Pythagorean synthesis."

"Pythagorean? As in the Greek philosopher?" Vesta asked.

"One and the same. You see, he originated the correlation between the seven musical notes. I mean, they already existed, but only by ear. Our ancient ancestors chose the notes because the sounds resonated within them. That was my first inkling of what was possible. This was before they knew anything about science or physics. Pythagoras was the first to explain it mathematically."

Vesta cocked her head.

"Don't worry," Liam said. "I didn't understand all of that either at first."

"You see, musical notes hold incredible power over our energetic system. During Medieval times the FB interval was called diabolical because some clergy claimed it caused feelings of lasciviousness."

"You don't want to get too randy in those gloomy old churches," Liam said.

"And in the fourth Century," Luc continued, "the Greeks believed Ionian harmonies encouraged heavy drinking."

"Those would have been my mates for certain," Liam said with a nod.

Luc turned toward the mixing board. "So, I began exploring what I could create with musical notes that would cause physical effects on us. In pleasant ways."

She pushed a few buttons and a tape machine in the corner begin rolling. A low hum began, a mild vibration in the room.

"Initially, my interest leaned toward sounds occurring in nature. That seemed like a logical starting point. But that quickly led to my interest in alchemy."

Liam looked toward Vesta as Luc explained.

"In fact, my record label is called First Matter because of my interest in identifying the seven whistles documented by a famous alchemist called Canseliet as he perfected the way to make gold. Each whistle as he was cooking the secret mixture of salt, Sulphur and mercury had a different tone according to his records. I wanted to know what notes they represented because that could translate to creating the building blocks of gold, in a manner of speaking, to our ears."

Vesta raised her eyebrows.

"Yeah, I know what you're probably thinking. I'm crazy, right?" She nodded her head. "At some point I decided the same thing, so I switched to learning how to tune our physical bodies."

Luc pushed a slider up on the mixing board. A higher octave started humming in the room along with a melody that reminded Vesta of something, but she couldn't remember what. An image began to waver on the periphery of her mind, almost on the tip of her tongue, nagging at her to say its name before it dissolved back into the shadows.

"So, I began taking yoga classes. Specifically, kundalini," Luc continued. "Do you know what I'm talking about?"

"Oh yes," Vesta said recalling her sunrise session with Amara and Guy in Tofino a year earlier.

"That's when I really struck gold!" Luc pushed two more sliders up on the board causing the vibration and melody to be mingled with a clear light voice making sounds rather than words and a violin echoing the notes of the singer.

"This is a plainchant melody in hexachords but I've added specific notes and rhythms that I've found resonate with our chakras. The voice is singing the mantra of each chakra in order from spine base to crown. And the Stradivarius seals the deal with its unparalleled tones."

The technicality of Luc's composition, the way she interwove her research of Pythagoras, kundalini, and alchemy was impressive, but all of that was superseded by the music itself. While it seemed born quite clinically, the result was anything but sterile. Vesta leaned back in her chair as the music swept over her. Her third eye began spinning like a roulette wheel. She closed her eyes to gain control as a surge of energy shot down through the top of her head to the base of her spine. It circled through every cell in her body and traveled up, exploding out through the top of her head.

"Ah!" She turned, loose of any restraint letting herself merge with the sound that she could now hear, see, taste, and smell.

A sensation of being vibrantly alive coursed through her. The thought occurred that her physical body might actually be floating above the chair, she wasn't sure and she didn't care. The only thing that mattered was that the flow continued because she could feel her pulse vibrating with the hum of the universe itself. Slower at first as a sea of red enveloped her, tinged with the seductive odor of earthy iron. It tasted like blood at its most elemental, vital, life-giving. Its thick vibration began to increase, changing color to a deep orange that smelled and tasted like ripe fruit. The rich liquid drenched her physical being. Sunshine, purer and more revitalizing than any she had ever felt before poured through her and overtook her senses with bright yellow and the zesty flavor of fresh air.

"Air has a taste?" some part of her asked.

Before the aspect of her logical mind could begin factoring such a concept, the color within her—around her—shifted to a summer green and tasted like love. Understanding that every particle that was ever created connected to every other particle forming a vast whole opened her heart, or what she could only describe in her limited vocabulary as her emotional center. There was no her, or them, only the abiding one. And it smelled like the bread Enid would pull from the oven on cold winter mornings.

Water gushed through her in the next moment and flooded

her senses with pale blue light that tasted cool, refreshing, and cleansing. It crystalized into a sense of clarity throughout the being known as Vesta giving her a voice to describe what she now understood.

"I allowed it to be blocked," she murmured.

From her third eye, pulsating a deep indigo color that smelled and tasted like the air from a window opened on a perfect spring morning, the image of Peter came into focus. His soft brown eyes locked onto hers. She broke into a smile as her heart unfurled petals of joy and love toward him. A tear rolled down his cheek.

"Help me Vesta," he said. "The Red King knows I hid it. He's going to kill me on unholy ground if I don't give it to him."

Vesta gasped her eyes flew open wide. The exquisite energy permeating every cell in her body vanished in a split second. The abrupt halt caused a sensation of being sucked into a black box—a cramped space so tiny that she could never possibly fit—to envelop her. She felt like she was suffocating. Her hands grabbed at her chest.

"I can't breathe," she stammered.

Liam sprang to his feet. "What's happening?"

"We have bottled water," Luc said as she bolted from her chair toward a small refrigerator by the door.

Vesta focused on her body, telling it to calm down. Managing her flesh and blood vehicle was of paramount importance. Regaining control of the basic system functions must come first. She visualized her physical form seeing what needed attention. Her energetic concentration moved to that area. Air began flowing into her lungs with easier breaths, the panic subsided.

She nodded her head. "I'm okay. But some water would be great."

Luc pulled a half empty bottle of Jose Cuervo tequila out of the refrigerator and sat it on the floor. She reached further back and grabbed a bottle of Evian. After unscrewing the top, she handed it to Vesta.

"Are you okay?" Liam asked. "Should I call a doctor?"

"No." Vesta shook her head. "I'll be fine." She took a sip of water. "I don't know what happened."

Luc gave Vesta a quick glance as she sat down in her chair again. "I think I do."

She turned the music off and swiveled to face her. "It's the music. The specific tones along with the sounds associated with each chakra. They open you up." Luc spread her arms out to visually emphasize what she meant. "Especially for sensitive people, like you."

"I saw Peter," Vesta said. "He's in trouble." She looked at Liam as she ran her fingers through her short blonde hair. "You were right." She looked down at the floor.

Liam exhaled. "Where is he?"

"I didn't see any location. It was dark all around him except for his face. He was crying."

Vesta wanted to cry too, but instead she stood up. She unconsciously curled her right hand into a fist. "He said someone was going to kill him on unholy ground."

"That means he's not at the Chartres labyrinth," Liam said.

"And he said the Red King knew he hid it, and was going to kill him if he didn't get it." Vesta stared at Liam. "What is he talking about?"

"The Red King?" Luc said leaning forward in her chair toward Vesta. "That could be an alchemical term." She held her hand up. "Sorry to interrupt but as I said, I took a deep dive into studying that."

"Go on," said Liam.

"Well, in simple terms, it's the metaphorical union of the

Red King and the White Queen that creates what's known as the great work, or turning any base metal into gold."

"Wait," Vesta said. "Alchemy is some faux science dreamed up by guys five hundred years ago. Right? There's no factual basis for any of that."

"I don't know. The books I read in my stepmother's private library made a big deal about it." Luc shrugged her shoulders. "It seemed like somebody figured out how to do it."

"Or it could be totally unrelated to that. It could mean that someone is nicknamed the Red King. Some mob boss maybe." She looked at Liam. "What do you think?"

"Can you see anything else with your InSight?"

Vesta rubbed her temples, then her third eye. "I'm trying but I always need some recovery time in between." She exhaled and shook her head. "It takes a lot of steam out of me when I generate that much energy."

She began pacing in the studio. Since she had begun learning how to tap into her InSight six months earlier, she had developed not only an adeptness for it but had discovered a way to access it on demand. If she focused on a subject, even if it was something as broad as the Amazon rainforest, for example, she would pick up anything that felt contrary to the flow of the natural order.

That was how she helped Amara find the poacher there who was killing jaguars and also killing members of the local tribe who were trying to stop him. She was able to describe the location where he was hiding, and the Brazilian police worked from the landmarks she specified to find and capture him.

Why could she focus on such a general subject and locate a random target so easily with her InSight but didn't see earlier that Peter needed her?

"Because I allowed it to be blocked," she said out loud to the others, but mainly to herself. The recollection caused her to freeze mid-step.

"What did you say?" Liam asked.

"That's what happened. Why I couldn't see Peter earlier."

"You did say something to that effect when you were in your trance, or whatever you call it," Liam said.

Vesta sat down and leaned her head back against the chair. Anger and embarrassment flooded through her. How could she have been so confident that she mastered InSight—regained all her power—that she allowed something to slip past her, blocking it without her even realizing it? Especially when it could mean the murder of someone she deeply cared about.

Confidence was an attribute that set winners apart from those who never succeeded at their goals or those who simply got lucky once in a while. Vesta recognized that early in her life. It was confidence in her abilities that led to her rise to the top of Sybarite. And to relearn the mastery of InSight to be of service to the planet and all the beings on it. But it was also her confidence running unchecked that allowed something to block it where Peter was concerned. She knew a balance must be struck and that her ability to connect with Peter remain strong.

"I have to go to his labyrinth." She stood up. "Immediately." She paced around the studio again.

"But he isn't in Chartres. You said so yourself." Liam stood up and began pacing with her. "You must locate where he is so we can send Cyrus in to get him."

Vesta stopped walking and put her hands on her hips. "I don't need Cyrus. I can handle it."

She wouldn't give in to her previous failure. Her InSight for Peter had returned so she could rescue him and make amends for her arrogance, her stupidity.

"He's been kidnapped!" Liam pleaded. "You heard what he said."

"When I find him, I'll call the police."

"Because that plan worked out so well last time in Key West."

Vesta shot a glance at him that could melt the rings on his fingers. "That was different."

"How?"

"I wasn't up to speed with my InSight. I am now."

Liam began shaking his head. "You need some back up."

Luc raised her hand. "Excuse me. Sorry to butt in again, but I'm heading to Paris tomorrow to stay with my parents for a few days before I go to Italy. You could come there and I could explain to my father what has happened. He's very well connected with the French authorities. I'm sure he could introduce you to a police captain or something. That might help."

Vesta began to nod her head. An introduction like that could open a more personal channel and keep law enforcement at bay until she needed them.

"Good idea," she said as she walked toward the door.

"Tell me why you're going to Chartres. You know he isn't there." Liam's demanding tone was unusual for him and caught her a bit by surprise. She paused and studied his face for a moment.

"Because his energy saturates that cathedral. If I go there, I will be able to see exactly where he is now."

"I hope you're right," he said. "Because bad things happen when he dies somewhere else."

Chapter Three

"I'm coming with you," Sandor said.

"No. I can, and want, to do this on my own."

"The hell you can." Sandor walked into Vesta's kitchen to make another cocktail.

She liked the fact that her apartment was only one-thousand square feet. There was no unnecessary space. The only bedroom opened to the kitchen and living room. It was her private enclave which by design couldn't accommodate any overnight guests unless she invited them into her bed. Sandor in her bed made her happy, but she insisted he keep his own apartment.

"Someone has committed a felony crime of kidnapping and is threatening murder." He waved his highball glass at her. "Do you really think you can tangle with someone like that single-handedly?"

"I'm not going to physically overpower them. After locating where Peter is, I'm going to bring in help."

The doorbell rang.

"That's them," he said.

Vesta walked into the kitchen area and opened the door for Amara and Jared.

"Big surprise," Sandor said as they entered. "She doesn't want our help."

"It sounds like there's no need to ask how you are," Jared said.

Amara leaned in toward Vesta to hug her but she dodged it with a quick buss on her cheek.

"We're fine," she said. "I need to pack. My flight leaves at six-thirty in the morning."

"Wait," Jared said. "Give us a rundown on what has happened so far."

"I thought Sandor told you on the phone."

"He did," Amara said. "But it would be good to hear it from you since it was your InSight that located him."

Vesta exhaled long and loud, mildly irritated because she felt it was a waste of time to repeat what they already knew. "I saw Peter crying. He called me by name and asked me to help."

She turned away from the trio swallowing the lump that unexpectedly popped up in her throat. Pausing a moment as the vision replayed in her mind, the acknowledgment that he suffered because of her ineptitude was gut-gnawing. Hard blinks pushed back the tears as she cleared her throat.

"He said that the Red King was going to kill him if he didn't give him what he had hidden." Vesta turned back to face the trionfi and raised her hands. "I have no idea what that means."

Amara looked at Jared who shook his head. "You know that was moved a long time ago."

"What?" Vesta asked.

"The ark," Amara said.

"The ark?" Vesta cocked her head. "Like Noah's ark?"

Amara smiled. "The Ark of Covenant."

Vesta's eyebrows peaked on her forehead. "The box with the ten commandments?"

"It's much more than that," Amara said. "But, yes."

"That was at Chartres Cathedral?"

"Centuries ago," Jared said.

"The Templars took it there to hide after they discovered it in Jerusalem. That's why they coughed up so much dough to have the place built." Sandor picked up his fresh scotch on the rocks and pointed at Vesta. "You knew that at one point since you were the architect."

Vesta stared at him stone-faced for a moment. "Yes," she said finally. "We all know I put a spell on myself and wiped my memory clean." She turned her attention to Amara and Jared. "But let's stay focused on today. Do you think whoever kidnapped Peter is thinking the ark is still there?"

Jared shrugged. "Hard to say."

"Whoever is holding him is convinced he knows the hiding place of something important," Amara said. "I haven't heard of anyone seriously looking for the ark in a very long time."

"Has Peter mentioned to either of you that he hid something of great value?"

Sandor shook his head. "Not me. But we haven't needed to talk much this time.

"Who is this Red King? Maybe we should start from there," Amara said.

"I have no clue," Vesta said.

"Any ideas?" Jared looked at Sandor.

"Nope," he said. "Never heard of him."

"Can you tap into your InSight again to find out who he is," Amara asked.

"I've tried," Vesta said. "It's really strange because I didn't have any indication from it that Peter was in trouble. Then

Liam asked me about him that night at Le Bernardin when he told me he was missing from the cathedral."

"How long?"

"Almost a month. Then I went to the studio to listen to the new music that he and Luc are making, and the Peter InSight hit me."

"What music?" Amara asked.

"This experimental stuff that Luc says activates your chakras."

Amara's eyes lit up. "Really?"

"A lot of basic tones and chants mixed in with a melody of some sort."

"It sounds amazing."

"It sent me on a magical mystery tour for sure. I thought I was floating around the room."

"Maybe you were," Amara said, her eyes sparkling.

"Anyway, that's when the InSight with him happened. It shocked me so much to see Peter begging me for help that I think it broke the connection." Vesta looked down at the floor. "Maybe I would have seen where he was if I had held it longer."

"Don't beat yourself up, kid. Want a drink?" Sandor asked.

Vesta shook her head. "I need to pack then lay out some instructions for Jenny and the rest of my staff by email while I'm gone."

"I'm going to come with you. You know that, right?"

"Look, just because you have a key to my apartment now doesn't mean you own me."

"Hey," Sandor said putting his hands up. "You are your own woman. We all know that. I'm just trying to help."

"Well, thanks but no thanks."

Sandor picked up his drink from the counter. "Let me put it to you like this. You can't stop me from getting on that flight in the morning because you don't own me either. And it would be in the best interest of Peter if you work with me on this."

Vesta stared at Sandor but said nothing.

"We need to alert the proper authorities in France that you're going to be calling them," Jared said.

"I have that covered. I'm meeting Javier Garcia at his house in Paris tomorrow. He knows who to contact."

"Javier?" Amara said.

"Yeah, Luc suggested it."

Sandor nodded toward Amara. "I told her that Javier is all about the Benjamins and to be careful."

"Yes, but he's been so generous to my foundation. While he does make a lot of money, he gives a lot of money too."

"True," Jared said. "But I have to agree with Sandor, Javier can con the bark off a tree."

"If he can help me by getting police backup there when I need them, then everything will be fine. I know how to handle con men."

Vesta began walking toward her bedroom, but stopped. "By the way, Luc mentioned her stepmother. Who's her biological mother? And did she divorce Javier?"

"Now that's a story," Sandor said. "You may have read about it in the news a few years ago."

"His first wife became very successful as a fitness expert," Amara said. "She was the founder of Peak Fitness."

"Remember all those gyms around the city for a while?" Sandor asked. Vesta nodded. "Well, she started them. Produced all those videos with celebrities."

"Xuxa was a powerhouse and had a lot of vision for where she wanted her business to go before she died," Amara said.

"Xuxa? I've never heard that name before," Vesta said.

"It's very old. From the Basque region. Where she and Javier came from originally," Amara said.

"It means lily in that language," Jared said. "So, she went by Lily in public to make it easier."

"How did she die?"

"Plane crash," Sandor said. "It nose-dived into the Atlantic with her and her lover onboard."

"That's rumor," Amara said.

"It's true and you know it."

"Oh, I remember something about that," Vesta said. "About ten years ago. It was a private plane, right?"

"Yep, dropped like a rock from the clear blue sky," Sandor said.

"It was eight years ago, and Javier set up a foundation in her memory a year after that. It's one of our biggest benefactors now."

"And his new wife?"

"Grace. She's lovely too," Amara said. "She's not Basque, but she comes from French heritage."

"Another interesting story," Sandor said. "Even more intrigue in her family."

"You'll have to save it for another time. I'm going to pack. Amara, Jared, help yourself to whatever you want here in the kitchen, although the only things you'll probably find are vodka, coffee and sparkling water. I'll let you know when I find Peter."

Vesta walked into her bedroom and closed the door. She pulled her custom-made Sybarite suitcase out of the closet. May in France meant temperatures could still be chilly, especially at night, with decent chances of rain almost every day. Sybarite sweater sets were the perfect choice to match with any trousers. She drummed her fingers on the luggage. Her thoughts wouldn't stay focused on any more clothing details. Each one led her back to Peter.

He must have tried to connect with her repeatedly after he was kidnapped. Nausea welled up inside her when she envisioned the black wall he must have hit when he tried. A twinge of guilt sprang up when she thought of Liam too. When he voiced his alarm at Peter being absent from Chartres, she dismissed it. Liam was the only person who felt like family to her now that Uncle Raymond was dead. She wanted to be someone he could always turn to when he needed help, but she hadn't listened to him when she should have.

Vesta stroked the necklace laying around her neck. Never would she have chosen it for herself. The odd-shaped stones, lacking congruity of a color palette, unpolished with scratches from years of abuse strung together with a new sterling silver crescent moon hanging from it would be a challenge to pair with any of her outfits. But Liam gave it to her asking for her to wear it all the time. And she would honor that, at least for the foreseeable future. If it lay discretely underneath her clothing, it would still be keeping her promise.

She walked to her chest of drawers and pulled out three Hermès scarves. Perfect for covering the misshapen necklace and shielding her neck from any chilly breezes. From the closet she selected several pairs of trousers, skirts and shirts, plus a couple of Chanel dresses. The hurried collection would give her many options for her wardrobe lasting at least a week in France, or wherever she needed to go.

The murmur of voices in the kitchen subsided followed by the familiar sound of her front door opening then closing. Sandor walked into the bedroom.

"I'm going home to pack."

"You really don't need to go to Paris with me."

"Yes, I do. You don't know what you'll face once you dive into this. Your InSight could fail again."

Vesta dropped her scarves into the suitcase. "I won't let that happen."

"Hm," Sandor said cocking his head. "It's already happened once without you realizing it."

"That's because I'm new at this." She began rolling up a pair of trousers. "Relearning it all. Don't give me a hard time."

"I'm not. I'm trying to help."

Sandor slid his arm around her waist.

"I just got you back in my life," he said. "The way we used to be. I'm not going to lose you yet because of your stubborn reliance on doing everything yourself."

He kissed her neck. "I know how you operate. But you're not ready to take on something like this yet. The consequences are too big."

Vesta slid her eyes toward him. "Are you talking about something else than Peter dying?"

She placed the trousers inside her luggage then faced him. "Because Liam said something tonight about bad things happening when Peter dies some place other than in the cathedral. Do you know what he meant? He wouldn't tell me. He said he couldn't talk about it yet. Which is very unusual for him." Vesta shook her head. "But he's been acting strangely since dinner the other night."

A shadow moved across Sandor's chestnut-colored eyes bringing a seriousness to them she had never seen before.

"That's because it was so bad the last time, especially for him."

"What do you mean?"

Sandor walked to the window in her bedroom staring out over the sawtooth skyline.

"During the early days of the second world war, he was a performer in a cabaret show in Berlin. Very popular with the Third Reich upper brass. Especially Göring. Peter had escaped to Mont Saint-Michel along with some other priests just before the Nazis invaded Chartres. American troops planned to bomb the cathedral because they thought the Germans were using it as an observation post. A colonel named Griffin took an enlisted man with him inside on the mission of checking it out and proving that it wasn't. That man was your father and he was desperate to save the cathedral for Peter and for you. He planted the thought in Griffin's mind. They reported back to their commander that it wasn't an outpost and the cathedral was spared. Later that day they were both killed in the town of Lèves. Forty-eight hours after that Chartres was liberated by the Americans."

Chill bumps raced over Vesta's body. She opened her mouth to speak but stopped. Sandor continued to gaze out the window.

"Liam by that time was living in Paris and went to Mont Saint-Michel to get Peter to return him to Chartres. They were caught by the Nazis in Rouen. Peter was killed on the steps of Saint Ouen Cathedral trying to get inside. Liam was accused of being part of the French Resistance, which he was, and of being a homosexual which he also was then. They sodomized him, tortured him then hacked his body into pieces and threw them into the Seine. Rouen was liberated by French forces three days after that."

"Oh my God," Vesta stammered. "No."

Sandor looked down running his finger along the windowsill. "With Cyrus, Liam and Enid—whose death you remembered a few months ago—gone, Rasputin was able to run totally unleashed with his new amusement of promoting Communism in his Russian homeland. But more devastating was Peter's death."

He turned to face her. "Even though he doesn't seem to take an active role, like the rest of us in policing world events, being that he's almost always in the cathedral, Peter actually does. You see, almost two thousand years ago, when we were all quite new at our jobs that the Elders gave us, Peter rose to the height of his gift. The Elders understood that humans required a spiritual base. They recognized that we had already created pantheons of gods, not only to explain things in nature but to fill up our souls with purpose and direction. That was Peter's job."

"Maintaining a healthy sacred connection, is that what you're saying?"

"Yeah," Sandor nodded. "It's as important as anything else we do for the RanChan."

Vesta wrinkled her nose.

He shrugged. "That's not a respectful name for them, I know. It's just an easy reference." He leaned against the window frame. "It was during that time that Peter met the man who, to this day, is his spiritual master."

"You mean Jesus."

"Exactly. His teachings resonated with Peter. All of his spiritual boxes were checked. So, after Jesus was crucified Peter devoted the rest of that life to continuing the spiritual doctrine he had laid out. And became the founder of what we now know as the Catholic Church."

"Upon this rock I will build my church," Vesta said.

Sandor pointed his finger at her and winked. "Yep, Peter carried out the request. But because he is who he is, like we all are, human to begin with, possessing our own innate personalities before we received our gifts, Peter always felt there was more for him to learn and understand. He explained to me that Jesus was no longer in physical form, he had merged with the Divine, God, whatever name you choose. But through meditation, prayer, he could tap into his energy once again."

Walking from the window, Sandor took Vesta's hand. "He roamed for a thousand years after that. His spiritual angst echoing around the world manifesting a very dark time for humanity as he sought more understanding. See, when his spiritual balance is off, out of kilter, the RanChan," Sandor winced.

"The humans, are affected by it and their own spiritual balance goes out of whack."

"That's when malevolent energies like Raz jump in to take advantage of it."

"You got it." He smiled at her. "When you designed the Chartres Cathedral you created a metaphysical, as well as a physical, home for Peter. A place that you soaked in his energy with all the sacred geometry you knew how to use." Sandor raised his eyebrows. "Powerful stuff that humans feel on a spiritual level but very few actually understand from a scientific basis."

"And when Peter dies there, he dies in peace."

"Bingo! It was really quite brilliant of you to come up with that solution."

Vesta pulled her hand away from Sandor's and returned to packing. "Now I understand. I'm rescuing not only Peter but the rest of the world from slipping into some spiritual abyss."

"We are."

"Don't you see?" She shot a quick glance at him. "I intuitively know what to do. You just said that."

"Hold on a second." Sandor reached for her arm but she moved it by picking up another pair of trousers to roll. "It's true you have this insanely powerful gift of InSight. And you and Peter have this spiritual connection, but running off by yourself half-cocked when you've just relearned how to use your gift is crazy."

He reached for her arm again taking hold of it gently but firmly. "We work as a team. I know you're not used to doing that in this life, but that was the wisdom of the Elders. That's where they went wrong on their trial run with the First Bloods."

She had heard the story of the First Bloods who all possessed the same gifts. And how their individual lusts for power caused them to slaughter each other except for Valentina who was the last one standing.

Sandor was right, she wasn't accustomed to working in partnership with others unless she was the leader, unless they followed her orders. She was the High Priestess, after all, imbued with InSight the others didn't have. It would be the only way she would agree for him to come with her.

"Okay, but you have to follow what my intuition tells me."

"Hey," Sandor peaked his eyebrows. "I have some damned good gifts too. Don't forget that." He pulled her into his arms. "Being charming and persuasive are only a couple of them."

Chapter Four

The flight from New York was late due to fog in Paris. Landing a jet, the size of a seven-forty-seven in a thick cloud bank seemed like an impossible task, but the pilot did it without any problem. After they collected their bags Vesta and Sandor took the train to Montparnasse then connected to another that stopped in Chartres. They rolled their luggage from the station past the little shops and up the street. When they arrived at the park, they could see the cathedral dwarfing everything else within view. The Mansard roof on the seventeenth century three-story building in front of them looked tiny by comparison. Behind that she could see the much older roofs of buildings from the fourteenth century. It was like rings on a tree as they walked from the modern world into the ancient.

"It's been a long time since I was here," Sandor said. "A few things have changed, but not much."

Vesta looked up at the mismatched spires soaring in the golden hues of the late afternoon sky. It felt like she was home. A long exhale slipped out of her mouth leaving her with a sense of calm. Anxiety had gnawed at her from the moment they landed but seeing the cathedral—knowing she would be inside of it soon—caused a wave of relief to spread through her. She and Peter were connected through that place. His energy was in every stone of it and so was hers. She would find him and he would be safe again.

They dragged their bags over the time-worn cobblestone streets as they approached their hotel, Le Parvis. Sandor pulled the door open for her and they walked inside. William was sitting behind the tiny reception desk where she saw him last six months earlier.

As she opened her mouth to say hello Sandor beat her to it. Much to her surprise he began speaking fluent French as well as any born and bred Frenchman she had ever heard. He checked them into the room that she had reserved, thanked William for the key and they headed up the old wooden spiraled staircase to the Henri IV chambre.

"I'm not surprised you chose this room."

"Why?" Vesta asked.

"Good king Henry was one of your favorite French kings. Aside from the fact that he was coronated here."

Sandor opened the door and Vesta walked in. "Well, that and the fact that it looks out toward the cathedral."

She dropped her bags. "I wish I could remember all those lives. The people I must have known."

"Better than that were the things you did," Sandor said as he placed his bag on the floor next to hers. "But you're still one hell of a woman even without all those memories."

"I'm amazed that you and the other trionfi can keep up with all those lives. Remember them, I mean."

"It's like looking back on one long life. You remember certain moments from childhood, some from each decade. You know what I mean? I've forgotten a lot, but most of us keep diaries that we pass on to ourselves to remember people, places, how we handled smaller events."

"Am I the only one who's cast a spell to forget? I can see how the stress could become overwhelming life after life. I mean, look what happened to Liam last time, for example."

Vesta shuddered.

"Yeah, we've all gone underground at some point, for sure, to take a break. But that's what the trionfi is really good at. We always look out for each other and when one is suffering burnout, we rally around to pull them out of their funk. Liam did cast a spell, one we call the Shock Absorber, when he realized what the psycho Nazi's planned to do to him. It wasn't a total wipe like yours, but allowed him to return this time without the full impact memory of how he went out."

"So that night at CBGB's when he OD'd on stage," Vesta began.

Sandor nodded. "He should have died but because of his spell it triggered an auto-response, of sorts. He bounced back with a full memory of who he was."

"I remember that night. I was standing in front of the stage when he hit the floor. He was gone, I swear. The look on his face. Then he just popped back up like nothing happened."

"That's the way the spell works. Turned out good for the rest of us because we needed him." He wrinkled his forehead as he glanced at her. "Especially since you were out of the picture for what we thought would be this whole life."

Sandor walked over to the large window and stared at the cathedral for a moment. "Those Elders were smart. They figured out how to divvy up our gifts, so we had to rely on each other, and help each other."

Vesta set her handbag on the sofa.

"I want to hear more about this but first I'm heading into the cathedral to see if I can find any clues from Peter."

"I'll come too."

"No. I want you to stay. Your energy might distract me."

"Fine. I'll go down to that medieval grain cellar they call a lounge here to see what kind of scotch they have. Being this close to the U.K. they might have something decent."

Vesta walked across the cobblestone rue du Cheval Blanc and up the sidewalk to the north portal, also known as the port royal. The now familiar medieval kings and queens carved out of stone and stuck on the columns stared down at her. She was used to their reproving gazes and saluted them as she walked up. The notion struck her that she probably knew the people when they were alive. Even more, she guessed they were delighted to be ensconced there for eternity to give scolding looks to all the infidels who passed by.

As she pulled open the first small wooden door then the second, she heard the grand chords of the organ. Mass was underway. Being that it was Tuesday, the labyrinth was closed, parishioner's chairs sat on top of it until Friday. The sun had dipped below the landscape of restaurants and shops to the west plunging all the soaring stained-glass windows into silent darkness for the remainder of the day. Bare bulbs dangling from long cords along the sides of the nave were the only illumination except for the transept where the mass gathered.

Traces from Peter's kidnapping must be somewhere in the cathedral. She had to find them. Vesta walked down the south aisle pausing at the zodiac clock carved from stone at the start of the rood screen. Two sculpted angels on either side were proudly presenting it to all passersby. Roman numerals counting to twelve twice ringed the circumference. A fat crescent moon phase and a dark field of stars were painted next to a pantheon of astrological characters, some painted red, others black, and still others white.

"Many visitors are aghast at the zodiac being so prominent

here in a Catholic church," a female voice with an English accent spoke at close range.

Vesta whirled around to see a stocky woman of about seventy dressed in a drab gray sweater and skirt standing close by.

"Pardon me," Vesta said.

"The zodiac," the woman pointed toward it. "When this cathedral was built almost a thousand years ago the zodiac was so accepted that even the pope had a personal astrologer."

"Oh, right. I actually knew that already."

"It's only been in the last few hundred years that astrology was cast in a negative light. A plot by the priests to gain more power."

"Oh," Vesta said as she appraised the woman. While she was dowdy on the best of days with her gray hair pulled back into a neat bun, her blue eyes twinkled like sapphires when she spoke.

"The real history of course is down in the crypt. Have you been there yet?"

"No." Vesta fumbled for words. "I mean, not recently."

The woman smiled. "*Le Puits des Saints Forts* is there."

Vesta furrowed her brows. "The well of the strong saints?"

"That's right. That's where our lady underground is. You should go there."

"What is that?"

"It's where everything connects. As above, so below. Whatever falls from the sky we are able to gather in the deep of the ground." She pointed at the clock again. "The ones who painted those zodiac figures in the red, black, and white, they understood."

Vesta nodded as if she were focused on the woman's words but in reality, she had refocused on Peter. If he had even a few moments before departing the cathedral he would have left a clue about his kidnapping for her. She had to keep searching.

"Sounds interesting. I'll have to visit it some time," Vesta said trying to be polite as she walked toward the apse rubbing the tingling spot on her forehead.

The woman called after her. "Some people might be considered fools who go down there, but I guarantee it's worth your time."

"Okay. Thanks," Vesta said dismissively and with a tinge of irritation at having her focus interrupted. She needed to walk the rest of the cathedral before catching the seven o'clock train to Paris to see Javier Garcia. As she walked past the Chapel of Confessors and the entrance to the Chapel of Saint-Piat, she could hear the priest deep in his liturgy as his words echoed off the ancient stone walls. Nothing called to her intuitively as she took slow steps through the apse, yet the spot between her eyebrows was itching. That always meant she needed to pay attention. Her frustration level felt like a thermometer in the Mojave Desert. She couldn't zero in on exactly what needed her awareness.

Past the Chapel of Martyrs and the Sacristy, she stopped at the Chapel of Notre Dame du Pilier and gazed at the shrine. Mary and her holy baby stared back in silence. Their ebony faces beneath golden crowns remained unmoved by her anxiety.

"What is it I'm supposed to pick up on?" She glanced around herself. "I know there is something, but I can't locate it." Her beseeching tone fell on their deaf wooden ears.

At the transept she paused to watch the mass for a few moments. The priest and parishioners went through their ritual oblivious to her. Scripture and prayers in French of God's love and the necessity of devotion uttered in somber voices. Peter, neither physically nor energetically, was present. Pursing her lips together she looked around the vast space for a sign, any sign. Only shadows growing larger and deeper by the moment were present. She walked past her imprisoned labyrinth to the little wooden door at the royal portal, pushed it open, pushed the second little wooden door to the exterior open, and stepped into the cool of the early evening. Her mission was not accomplished but she and Sandor had to catch the train.

The ten-minute walk to the station was made in silence. Vesta needed time to think. How would Peter leave a clue or a message for her? Had she missed something? Maybe he didn't have the chance to leave one. On the periphery of her awareness something tugged at her like a thread trying to unravel. She needed to shake it loose, something wanted to come through. After choosing a seat by the window, with Sandor taking the aisle seat next to her to chase away any interference, she closed her eyes to call forth her InSight. Using the technique she perfected months earlier, she called upon it. Nothing happened. She commanded herself to relax and focus more, let her mind go blank of distracting thoughts. Heavy weights wrapped around the needless thoughts were dropped into the cosmic ocean to disappear. She waited in the void. Impenetrable blackness clung to her. It stank like soured milk. No sight, no sound came forth. A deep frown dug into her forehead as she opened her eyes.

She glanced at Sandor who was reading the day's issue of *Le Monde*. There was no way she would tell him her InSight had failed. He warned her it might. Something blocked it again despite Luc's music clearing it away. That was the blackness she saw which felt like sticky mud. She knew she needed the chakra-opening sounds once more to dissolve the barrier. Vesta smiled to herself. It was fortuitous they were headed that way. She would banish the block forever with Luc's help and Sandor would never know any difference.

In Paris, they took a cab from Montparnasse to Avenue Montaigne. The Garcias lived in a *hôtel particulier* in the toney eighth arrondissement near the Champs-Élysées. As they turned into the area known as the Golden Triangle, Vesta noticed Horse Chestnut trees, tiny sparkling white lights glittering on them, lining the streets. Raindrops from a shower, hours earlier still clinging to the window glass of the taxi created a softening effect on the scene as she gazed at it. Surreal and romantic, with the black night as a backdrop, it reminded her of a Paris photograph taken long ago. Savoring the moment, appreciating its enchantment—the kind only Paris could create—she deeply understood, in that instant, her need to never lose the ability to recognize and cherish that kind of magic. How essential it was for that connection to her old self to remain. The taxi pulled to the curb, and they got out.

A wave of energy she could only describe as being on a choppy sea in a tiny boat washed over her when she placed her feet on the steps to the main door. On impulse she grabbed Sandor's arm to steady herself. Silently she lambasted the move.

"What's wrong?" He stopped to look at her.

Any appearance of weakness was unforgivable. "Nothing, my heel slipped on the step." She turned loose of his arm and smoothed her hair behind her ears. "I'm fine now."

"You sure?"

"Yes. Ring the bell." Calling upon the calming techniques she learned from Amara's kundalini sessions to steady her body and mind, she slowly inhaled to the count of eight, held the breath for four counts then released it over four counts. The energetic turbulence began to subside.

Sandor pressed button five, and a buzzer sounded unlocking the door to the street. They walked to the lift and took it to the fifth floor. When the door opened Javier stood ready to greet them wearing a well-cut Balenciaga suit to match his trim black beard and mustache. His dark penetrating eyes pulling them into the room.

"Hello and welcome to my home. Please come in."

They followed him as he walked through a doorway, past a vestibule laid with white marble on the floor and walls into a room with soaring ceilings. The walls were also white, original nineteenth century moldings crowning the room's grand effect. A low, deep-tufted, black leather sofa and club chairs surrounded a red lacquered coffee table. Black marble surrounded a fireplace where a cozy flame danced inside. Above it hung a curious painting of a woman encased in a glass bottle. The effect was dramatic.

"I'm delighted to see you again so soon."

"Yes," Vesta said. "I appreciate you inviting us to your home on such short notice."

"It is not a problem at all."

"This is quite a place you have here," Sandor said looking around.

"You are too kind. You see, it was passed down to my wife, from her family. We have redecorated it to bring it more into the modern time." Vesta noticed how Javier's speech reflected both French and Spanish accents but there was some undertone to it that she couldn't quite place.

"Ah," he said. "And here she is now."

A woman dressed in solid white with Chanel trousers and a turtleneck sweater walked into the room. Her short wispy brown hair curled in soft cloud puffs around her face.

"Good evening," she said.

Javier stepped close and took her hand. "May I present Grace Garcia. My dear these are our honored guests Vesta Beauvais and Sandor MacFarland."

Grace smiled. "Hello. It is nice to meet you." Vesta noted her accent was pure French.

"Nice to meet you too," Sandor said.

"Hello," Vesta said.

"Please have a seat. May I get you a cocktail?" Javier asked.

"I would just like water with gas right now. Thanks," Vesta said.

"Do you have any scotch?" Sandor asked.

"Yes. Actually, I have some very nice scotch. But you tell me what you think."

Javier walked out of the room. Vesta and Sandor sat on the black leather sofa while Grace took a seat in one of the black club chairs across from them. An odd thought crossed Vesta's mind as she looked at the woman. She reminded her of the zodiac characters on the clock at the cathedral from earlier in the evening. Not because she resembled any of them. It wasn't that. She gazed at her a moment longer trying not to be rude. It was the colors, she realized, they were the same. Each of the zodiac characters was mainly either red, black or white. Grace sitting on the solid black leather chair in her white ensemble with the red lacquered table in front of her resembled those painted characters.

"Javier says he saw you at Le Bernardin in New York recently," Grace said breaking Vesta's train of thought.

"Yes, just a few days ago," Sandor said.

"He enjoys that place because Éric is from the Basque region," she said. "And a good cook as well." Grace laughed.

"Chef Ripert?" Vesta said. "I didn't know that. I'm friends, well a decent acquaintance, with him and he's never mentioned that."

"Not everyone wears their heritage as a badge as much as Javier."

She pointed to a painting on the wall. "If you notice the black symbol on the canvas."

"The one with the four swirling apostrophes?" Sandor asked. "Kind of like a boat propeller?"

Grace laughed again. "Yes, that is a good way to describe it.

That is the lauburu. It means four heads, and it is the symbol of the Basque people. It conveys the idea of unity and the uniqueness of their country."

"Basque is a region though. Not a country, right?" Vesta asked.

"Correct," Grace said. "But the Basque people think of it as a country."

"It's because of their language, isn't it? I read that Euskara is the oldest language in the world and completely different from any other in Europe."

"That is mainly correct, Ms. Beauvais, except that it is similar to a Celtic dialect."

"And that's because the Basque region was isolated geographically around the border of France and Spain by the Pyrenees Mountains."

Grace nodded her head. "I see you are well versed on the culture."

"Not really," Vesta said. "I think I read about it in a magazine on a flight somewhere."

"All of that is true. And my husband is very proud of his roots, as they say."

"And I should be," Javier said as he walked back into the room with a tray holding several glasses. "The purity of the culture has survived for thousands of years."

He set the tray on the red lacquered table.

"For you, your Highness." He handed Vesta her sparkling water.

"No Highness here," she said looking at Javier. "And no Ms. Beauvais either. Just Vesta," she said looking at Grace.

Javier placed a martini glass with a twist of lemon in front of his wife.

"And Dalmore '64 for you my friend," Javier said as he handed Sandor a high ball glass.

"For real?"

"I poured it from my Constellation Collection."

"Damn, that's a hundred grand worth of whiskey bottles there."

"And well worth it," Javier said.

Sandor brought the glass up to his nose and inhaled. Vesta watched a smile slide across his face.

"A toast," Javier said as he raised his own glass of whiskey. "To the occasion of the High Priestess and the Magician of the trionfi coming to our humble home."

"This isn't what I would call humble, but cheers," Sandor said.

"Javier said that you inherited this home," Vesta said looking at Grace.

"I did. It belonged to my grandmother Louise Barbe. How she came to own it is not clear. It passed to my mother who gave it to me."

"It's stunning," Vesta said.

"What is clear," Javier said. "Is that Madame Voronoff, her married name, was the subject of this historic artwork." He pointed to the oil painting hanging above the fireplace. "It is called *Le Vaisseau du Grand Oeuvre*, or The Vessel of the Great Work. She is magnificent."

On the canvas stood a voluptuous naked woman with dark hair and dark eyes encapsulated in what looked like a glass wine decanter which was filled to her knees in a watery liquid. She was proudly displaying a large jewel or stone on top of her head radiating red, blue and gold light from it. The dark blue sky depicted behind her had overtaken the setting sun leaving bands of pink, orange, and yellow close to the earth. A crescent moon and several planets including Saturn and Jupiter dotted the early night sky. Large crystals lay scattered on the ground around the woman with names written in an ancient-looking script clustered on the horizon.

"That's your grandmother?" Sandor asked with an approving nod.

"Yes, when she was quite young." Grace picked up her martini. "Unfortunately, hers was not a long life. She died after drinking potable gold."

"Potable gold?" Vesta asked.

"That is one theory," Javier said. "There are others. You see she was an alchemist, and that was—according to some—a failed experiment she attempted."

"Jean-Julien Champagne is the artist who painted it. More than likely he was the father of my mother," Grace said. "We don't know for sure."

"I think it is without question," Javier said. "She was divorced from Professor Voronoff for several years before she became pregnant."

Grace shrugged and sipped her martini.

"Nevertheless, Louise and then her mother passed down to Grace a wealth of books on the subject of alchemy."

"That's what Luc mentioned to me at the recording studio two nights ago," Vesta said trying not to sound too eager. "She mentioned that some of her music was inspired by it."

Javier snorted and uttered something under his breath that Vesta didn't understand and which didn't sound like English. She guessed it was in the Euskara language. Grace glanced away from Javier toward Vesta.

"I enjoy Luc's music," she said.

"Luciana has talent, it is true, but she should focus on creating a career, not these mindless pursuits," Javier said.

"I know she was very thoughtful in suggesting I meet with you about Peter's disappearance. Have you met him?"

"I have not," Grace said. "But I'm sorry to hear that he is missing."

"Have you?" Vesta looked at Javier.

He waved his hand dismissively. "Briefly. Once. He stays in that musty cathedral."

"Vesta was the architect you know," Sandor said.

"Yes, I read that in my diaries. Congratulations. You accomplished a great feat."

"Thank you. I'm anxious to get back to it and begin my search for him," Vesta began.

"Our search," Sandor interrupted.

"As soon as possible," Vesta continued. "Who do you suggest I call, which law enforcement group, when I locate Peter? When my uncle was murdered in Spain, Scotland Yard was there. Sandor and others had planned to take Rasputin into custody that night and so they were standing by."

"I am aware of that tragedy. My condolences for your loss. Let me give you my private mobile phone number. I will let my Scotland Yard contacts who are stationed here in Paris know that you are looking for your lost friend."

Javier pulled a pen and piece of paper from the inside of his jacket pocket. He wrote down his phone number and handed the paper to Vesta.

"Whoever is holding him captive is threatening to kill him."

"I understand your urgency," he said. "I will speak to someone tomorrow who will know exactly what to do. I will let you know."

"Thank you."

"Also, tomorrow there is a show of the fall collection from Balenciaga. Cristóbal Balenciaga was from Basque. He was a dear friend. A couturier's couturier. And I support his house even now as a custodian of his archives. I would be honored to have you as my guests. Grace will be there as well."

"I can't, but thank you for the invitation. Finding Peter is my only thought right now."

"I understand. Of course. I knew your business, besides the trionfi, was with Sybarite, therefore I assumed you would be interested."

"Normally I would. I think Nicolas Ghesquière shows great promise as the new creative director."

"I agree," Javier said.

"Is Luc here tonight?" Vesta asked wanting to move forward with the second reason for her visit. "I would like to thank her for suggesting we come see you."

"No, I'm afraid she is out with friends." Grace said. "But I will tell her of your gratitude."

Vesta glanced at Sandor then toward Javier who stood beside Grace's chair. The next words she chose carefully, not wanting to appear desperate. "I was hoping to listen to her music again tonight. It really is quite inspiring to me."

"She has some discs in her room, I think. I could play one for you," Grace began.

"No!" Javier barked. "Those sounds are trash. I don't want them played in my home."

Sandor raised his eyebrows. "Harsh words for your daughter's efforts."

"She wastes her time on that nonsense."

"I was quite moved by it," Vesta persisted. "And I would love to hear more."

Grace glanced up uncomfortably at Javier whose only facial movement Vesta noticed were his dark eyes slicing a stern look in return. Grace blinked in acknowledgement and stood up. "I will tell her of your gracious words."

Sandor drank the rest of his scotch and set the glass on the red lacquered table. Vesta stood up knowing that any further attempt to hear the music would not only be futile but add to the thick, sticky energy which had blasted into the room.

"That was one hell of a decent whiskey." Sandor knew it too. "Thank you, but we must be going. We've taken up enough of your time."

"Yes," Vesta said. "It's been a long day and we are staying in Chartres tonight."

"We were happy to greet you in our home. Please, return any time." Javier's voice had regained its elegant, easy tone as he walked toward the entry door.

Grace stepped toward Vesta extending her hand. "It was a pleasure to meet you."

"Yes, nice to meet you as well."

She turned to Sandor. "Best wishes on finding your friend."

"Thanks. Looks like we'll need it."

Vesta and Sandor walked to the lift. Javier stood watching them as the door closed. She glanced toward Sandor to speak but he slipped his hand in hers and wiggled his finger for her to stop. She complied. They walked from the lift, down the hallway to the front door. Once outside as he looked for a taxi Sandor said, "He probably has the lift bugged."

"What?"

"Seriously. I don't trust that guy."

"Why? Because he doesn't enjoy his daughter's music?"

"It's a hunch I have. And I'm usually right about those things."

"But he has offered to help me with his Scotland Yard contacts."

"Yeah, I'll believe it when I see it."

Sandor waved down a taxi, and they got in.

"Montparnasse," he said to the driver. "And what's up with this alchemy thing? Did you notice their entire living room was red, black and white?"

"And so? What does that mean?"

"Those are the main colors represented in the process of what they call the great work."

"The great work? Like the name of the painting?" Vesta cocked her head.

"Yeah. And he seemed a little obsessed with Grace's grandmother didn't you think? I mean, she was hot, very hot, but it's your wife's grandmother."

"Maybe he was just proud to have a famous family member."

Sandor rolled his eyes. "I have a feeling there's more to it."

"Well, I don't care. I need to focus on finding Peter."

They arrived in the station at Montparnasse. A train to Chartres was scheduled to depart ninety minutes later.

"We have time for a glass of wine," Sandor said after he purchased the tickets. "I know a brasserie around the corner that used to be one of our favorites in the twenties."

"You mean the nineteen twenties?"

"Yeah. It was pretty rough around here in the eighteen twenties. Hugo used to call it the strange place no one knows."

"Hugo who?"

Sandor laughed. "Victor."

"You mean the guy who wrote Les Misérables and The Hunchback of Notre-Dame?"

"Sure. Old drinking buddy then. You knew him. In fact, I'm pretty sure you were the inspiration for Esmeralda." He pointed to the necklace she was wearing, the one Liam had given her. "Back then you wore a necklace with an emerald hanging from it. I remember you said that it kept your heart open so you could do a better job."

Vesta shook her head. "I don't have any of those memories." She knew they were lost in her current life, and maybe forever.

The only mindset she could embrace was looking forward. No further regrets.

"I'm kind of glad. It seems like a lot to keep up with."

Sandor took Vesta's hand and kissed it. "Ah, but we had some good times here. Walking on the Quai Voltaire browsing the book stalls, spending Sunday afternoons at the Louvre, then I would take you to dinner and the theatre."

Vesta smiled. "It sounds lovely."

Sandor smiled in return. "It was."

Her thoughts returned to Peter. He must have been walking the labyrinth in those days too. Did she visit him then? A knot twisted in her stomach as she thought about the misery he had to be in now. And the fact she couldn't see him with her InSight. She knew what she had to do as soon as they arrived at their hotel.

Chapter Five

All restaurants in Chartres were closed by the time their train arrived at the station near midnight. Vesta and Sandor took the short walk up the street toward the cathedral and in through the second-floor door to Le Parvis with their key.

"I'm going to the kitchen to find some bread and cheese," Sandor said. "Want to come with me?"

"No, we ate at the brasserie."

"Six snails swimming in butter doesn't cut it as dinner for me. I'll be back."

"What if everything is locked up?"

Sandor wiggled his fingers. "Magician, remember?"

Vesta shook her head as she walked into the Henri IV suite. She exhaled long and hard as she gazed at the cathedral through her window. No progress had been made locating Peter. She hadn't found a clue, and no InSight had come to her since listening to Luc's music. As she drummed her fingers on the window pane, she knew there was only one option left.

Tarot cards hadn't played an essential role so far in her seeing the future or what was currently hidden from her view that could have negative effects. That came through her InSight. Instead they functioned simply as the story of her trionfi family drawn symbolically and cryptically on the seventy-eight cards. After Amara gave her the deck and taught her about the cards months' earlier, she had established the habit of carrying them with her on trips. For some reason, unknown to her, it felt like the right thing to do so she followed the intuitive ping.

She pulled her suitcase onto the bed. Inside the lingerie storage compartment was the small zippered bag which held her cards. It was decorated with an image of the High Priestess card from the Waite-Smith deck printed on one side. A small smile peeked through her serious thoughts. Thousands of bags like that had been mass produced and sold over the years. Little did the manufacturer know that one day the actual High Priestess of the tarot herself would purchase one to hold her own cards.

The soft bag felt good in her hands as she unzipped it. A gentle warmth surrounded the cards as she pulled them out like they were humming with a subtle vibration. She walked to the low table in front of the sofa, sat down and began to shuffle. Lights illuminating the cathedral exterior reflected a pale-yellow glow through the window onto the deck. Several more shuffles of the stiff cards seemed necessary before she felt they were ready. She spread them out like a fan on the table and drew three cards quickly, without thinking, as Amara taught her to do. Hesitation in considering which cards to choose always interfered with intuitive guidance, Amara told her. Going with the first instinct, before her conscious mind could take over, would bring out the correct cards.

Vesta gasped as she laid the cards down one by one. The Hanged Man, the King of Pentacles and the Tower lay in front of her. She stared at them as a chill raced up her spine. The cards were speaking to her! The Hanged Man represented Peter. Last year he mentioned that the image on the card came from ancient times when he was hung upside down on a cross by men who were sent to kill him. The golden halo surrounding his head and the casual pose of one leg crossed over the other signified that not only was he agreeable with the position but that he knew he possessed the metaphysical capacity to transcend the earthly restraints if he chose to do so. Vesta touched the card. It quivered beneath her finger. Yes, it was communicating to her about Peter. And the spread was connecting him to the King of Pentacles.

Sitting on a throne, looking remarkably like he did in present times—minus the manicured facial hair—wealth and power symbols encircled him. In one hand was a scepter depicting power. The other held a large disc bearing a pentagram representing money. Behind him lay his sprawling castle. Dressed in a robe covered in flourishing green leaves safeguarding red ripe grapes, the king balanced a gold crown on his head. His ruby cowl protected his face. The Red King.

But Javier told her that he had met Peter only once. The spinning sensation began on the spot between her eyes. Vesta rubbed it. She knew it meant her third eye was activated by what she saw. It wasn't quite her InSight, but it was close. What did Javier have to do with Peter? Was he going to help her find him? Or was he involved in his kidnapping? No answer came, just an increasing heat as the little wheel between her eyebrows spun faster.

Her eyes moved to the third card, the Tower. A shiver ran through her. This card had appeared in the spread Madame Kali laid in front of her in her shop in Cairo. It was the first time Vesta had seen tarot cards up close, at least in this life. She had no idea what the image meant at that point. Flames were shooting out of a single gray tower as two people fell from it. Above, a lightning bolt zig-zagged down from the heavens toward the Earth on one side while a giant golden crown was being ejected from the top of the tower on the other side. It was a powerful symbol of change that was either coming or was underway. She knew that now.

Once the cards were identified and their meanings clear, Amara told her to examine the spread as a whole to understand the message. As she continued to study the three cards smoke began to trickle from the Hanged Man as it lay on the table. A flame popped up enveloping it, turning the corners brown and curling them over. She slammed her hand down on the card to extinguish the fire.

Panic ignited in every cell in her body but quickly turned into confusion when she realized she felt no heat from the fire. Her eyes widened when she lifted her hand to see the card untouched by any flame. No fire had burned it. It had been an illusion.

Vesta leaned back on the sofa and eyed the card. She saw it catch fire. But it didn't really catch fire. The message of the spread was clear. Peter was in mortal danger but she knew that already. She picked up the three cards.

"Tell me where he is," she said gliding the stiff cards between her thumb and fingers. She waited, repeating her demand for several minutes. No response came. Mild irritation at her failure evolved into a full-blown muscle in her back clinching up. She winced in pain and rubbed it with her fingers as she heard a muffled creak of wood.

Sandor walked through the door whistling When a Man Loves a Woman. He dropped an armful of things on the sofa next to her.

"What are you doing? What is that?"

"Your midnight snack I found in the kitchen. There's some brie and a baguette. And I discovered that William keeps the best wine hidden for himself in the pantry." He waved a bottle at her. "It's where everything connects in this place. As above, so below in that little cubby hole of his off the kitchen."

"What did you say?"

"I found some brie and,"

"No! The other thing you said. Where it all connects."

"Oh, that old alchemy saying. Javier got me thinking about it tonight," Sandor began.

"Tell me what that means!" Vesta almost shouted.

"What's got into you?"

Vesta slammed her fist onto the table. "Just tell me what that phrase means, as above, so below!"

"Alright. Alright. It's what the crazy dudes who thought they could turn metal into gold used to say. It's from the Emerald Tablet, meaning what's above in the heavens, metaphorically of course, is the same as below here on Earth, or within the soul of people."

Thunder crashed in her brain as her third eye sparked red hot. "That woman from the cathedral today, she was the clue. Or she was giving me the clue."

"What woman?"

"Never mind." Vesta walked to the window and looked toward the cathedral. "I need to get into the crypt."

"Tonight?"

"Yes."

"You can't. It's locked."

She pressed her fingers on the window pane for a moment then whirled around to face Sandor.

"You are the Magician in the tarot, aren't you?"

"You want me to break into Chartres Cathedral?"

"It's for a good reason. I think Peter is down there."

"In the crypt?"

"Yes."

Vesta and Sandor walked out of the second-floor door of Le

Parvis down to the cobblestone street. They walked in front of the royal portal entrance, around the corner to the south side of the cathedral by the apse. An old wooden double door painted a dark orange stood behind a rusted wrought-iron gate. Sandor pulled a ring of keys out of his jacket pocket. He sorted through several until his fingers landed on one. He moved close to the wrought-iron lock and inserted the key. Vesta heard a dull click, Sandor swung the door open, and they walked toward the wooden door.

"What are you going to do if they have a surveillance camera set up?"

Vesta wrinkled her forehead. "Do you really think anyone else would want to break into a dank crypt in the middle of the night?"

Sandor shrugged his shoulders and nodded. "Good point. Okay. Here goes."

He singled out another key from his collection and slid it into the lock on the door. After he wiggled it around for a minute, she heard the key turn and a bolt rattle releasing the door.

"I hope we can find the light switches," Vesta said.

Sandor shook his head. "You really have no idea who you're dealing with here, do you?"

He pulled two small flashlights out of his other pocket. She smiled as she took one and turned it on. They walked into the ancient crypt their lights cutting through the darkness to land on an ancient stone floor and wall. Vesta took several steps in then stopped. She shined her flashlight in an arc around her.

"Which way do we go to the well of the strong saints? Do you know?"

"Yeah, I do. It used to be on the outside of the church until you put it inside with your new plans."

"Hmm," Vesta murmured. "I wonder why I did that."

"You were tired of the Christian martyrs being thrown down the well."

Vesta shined her flashlight on Sandor. "Really?"

Sandor raised his eyebrows and nodded. "Yep. Seemed like a good solution."

"Okay. Which way?"

"Turn right," Sandor said. But Vesta walked straight toward a small room. "Where are you going?"

"I don't know, but I feel like I need to go here." The familiar warmth between her eyebrows sprung to life as the tiny wheel of energy began to spin again. As she waved the cone of light around her, Vesta realized she stood in a low barrel-vaulted space. A table covered with a white cloth was the only furniture in the room. A free-standing cross and simple candle holder were on top of it. The rest of the room was empty except for the fresco painted on the arched wall. Vesta shined her light on it.

"Ah, right. Figures that you would come in here," Sandor said.

"Why?"

"Because"—he pointed his flashlight at the tallest image painted on the wall—"this is the oldest depiction of Peter in the place."

Vesta gazed at the faded ancient mural of six saints, all their halos firmly in place, and someone who appeared to be a king sitting on a throne. "When was this made?"

"Eleven-hundreds. It's in the Romanesque style."

"What are they doing?"

"They're celebrating mass with Charlemagne. He was a big deal here because he gifted the supposed veil of the Virgin Mary to Chartres."

She smiled. "He looks the same today, doesn't he?"

"Who? Charlemagne?"

"No! Peter. That long face and timid expression. But the

eyes, even in this crude painting, his eyes still convey that wisdom and sadness, don't they?"

"If you say so."

Vesta whirled her flashlight toward him. "Why are you being so harsh?"

Sandor shook his head. "The guy who painted this didn't know what Peter looked like. At that point in history he had been dead a thousand years from his incarnation as Saint Peter. He was wandering in the forests around here with the Druids when this was done."

"He was a Druid?"

"Well, not really. He was just checking out what they believed in. All the nature spirits, that sort of thing. He's never strayed from his original connection." Sandor pointed at her. "You were the one who got him refocused when you built this place for him."

Vesta's throat tightened. She had to find him.

"Okay, where's the well?"

"On the other side of the gallery. Follow me." Sandor turned around pointing his light toward the door. "And really follow me this time," he said over his shoulder. "I'm ready to get out of this cold hole in the ground."

Vesta walked behind Sandor as they made their way through the passageway that curved to the left. Every few yards her flashlight would peer its light into another small chapel. She paused for a few moments at each one. Simple chairs lined up facing altars. Smooth, low groin vaults held the rooms together, silent and steadfast. On the walls she could barely make out scant faded medieval-style painted figures and ancient written words. No restoration had been attempted, instead they seemed destined to dissolve into history.

As they kept walking through the long, low tunnel it widened out to allow for an altar positioned in the middle of the space with a Madonna sitting on a simple throne, the baby Jesus perched on her lap holding what looked like a scroll in his hand. They appeared to be carved out of wood as her flashlight bounced off the polished surface of their darkened faces. A large crude-style tapestry rug stretched across the wall behind them, the light brown center clearly intended to frame the holy mother and child. Around the flame-shaped brown was a wide band of green which, in turn, was surrounded by a band of blue with patches of white mixed in.

"What's this giant needlepoint rug all about?" Vesta pointed to it. "Isn't it out of place down here? I mean it's definitely not ancient."

Sandor turned around and shined his flashlight toward her.

"That's the Madonna of the Underground. The brown part of the tapestry represents the earth, where legend says a black Madonna was discovered before a church was ever built here." He wiggled his light around the shrine as he spoke. "The green is the grass above the ground, with the sky above that."

He spun around to continue walking before he paused. "And also," he said as he turned to face her again. "It plays into the alchemy thing too. That whole as above, so below philosophy."

The flashlight pivoted back in the opposite direction away from her as Sandor began walking again. She looked toward the shrine hoping for a clue. Several moments passed as she stretched her psychic fingers out toward it begging for a sign. Yet the faces of the Virgin and her holy child remained placid. They would reveal none of their secrets to her that night.

Vesta exhaled and turned to catch up with Sandor when her light flashed into a little chapel containing a large arched stained-glass window, the sole feature in the room except for steps that led up to it. No chairs, just seven stairs that led nowhere except to a window which she was certain wasn't meant to open. It depicted no biblical scene as the ancient soaring windows did in the cathedral above. Instead, as her light shone on the stained-glass, she recognized the same colors from the tapestry in big glass shards of brown, green, blue and white converging into an abstract pattern echoing the alchemy concept Sandor mentioned a minute earlier. Intuitively, she understood the chapel and shrine were related to each other. But why build steps that led to a landing too narrow for anyone to stand on, at a window that has no view? She needed to decipher the clues.

"Sandor," she called out. His cone of light blazing forward in the tunnel pivoted back toward her.

"Are there a certain number of steps in the supposed process of turning lead into gold?" She asked.

"Yeah, seven. Why?"

Chapter Six

"We're almost through the ambulatory," Sandor said in an impatient tone as his pace sped up.

Vesta followed him while her thoughts raced along beside her. The British woman with the bright blue eyes specifically spoke about the well of strong saints in the crypt, but Vesta was sure that the alchemical symbolism of the Madonna and child as well as the chapel with the corresponding window and seven stairs was connected somehow to the puzzle. She also knew that Sandor was anxious to get to the well and then leave. There was no need to share her thoughts with him, but a picture was taking shape.

"Ambulatory," she said trying to ease his impatience, and hopefully his pace so she could get a better look at what she was walking past.

"I had no idea you knew anything about high Gothic architecture."

"Your constant chatter about it in those days rubbed off on me." He was several yards ahead of her and his words bounced off the stone walls into her ears from different directions creating a sort of stereo effect.

"And you still remember? How can you still remember after all the lifetimes you've had since?"

"Like I've said before, some stuff sticks." He looked back at her, his light sweeping toward her. "And it was important to you so it made an impression with me."

Vesta smiled. She had given Sandor such a hard time in this life. But he deserved it. Arrogant and so self-assured as one of the leading hedge fund brokers in New York, he could have any woman he wanted, and did. Their one dating experience years earlier had ended almost as soon as it started because she couldn't handle his egotism. Of course, then she didn't know she was the High Priestess of the tarot and he was the Magician and that they had been married in many lifetimes before.

"Did we ever have children?" The thought popped into her head and she surprised herself by asking it without hesitation.

"A few times, but not a lot. You were always focused on your job of sharing your InSight and serving the greater good. There were lives where you did nothing but that. You would be holed up in some castle for years. You're a hell of a lot more fun now. Okay, here we are."

Vesta caught up with Sandor and stopped beside him. Protruding from the stone and stucco wall was a demi-lune of a well housing. Her pulse quickened. Shining her light inside of it, all she saw was a bottomless black hole. Above it was an arch constructed of stone with something that looked like an oil lantern hanging from the center. Vesta scanned the lantern carefully on all sides with her flashlight. There had to be a clue from Peter.

"Shine your light around here too." The spot on her forehead began to spin.

Sandor moved his light all around the well. Their lights met and crisscrossed going over every inch of it as well as the wall and the arch.

"Maybe there's something inside the well," she said.

"If there is, you won't see it or find it. It's grated and it drops twenty or thirty feet down below that." Sandor shined his light down into the well but a gaping blackness swallowed it. "Peter wouldn't leave a message for you in there."

"But my third eye is buzzing like crazy. I know I'm on the right track."

"If you say so, your Highness."

"Stop it. Give me a minute." Vesta swept the flashlight slowly, meticulously over the well again even though she knew no messages were pasted, carved or drawn for her. She looked on the floor surrounding the well. Nothing lay there but the cold stones and a little pile of stucco rubble.

A long exhale slid past her lips. "Maybe I was wrong about the woman giving me a clue." She rubbed her forehead. "It's just that you came into the room saying exactly what she said. It's where everything connects. As above, so below. I was sure it was a sign." Vesta shook her head as she turned and took a few steps away from Sandor down the gallery.

"Can we go back to the room and have some cheese and bread now?" Sandor said. "I'm starving."

Irritation surged up her spine but as she whirled around to say something to him, her flashlight caught an image above the doorway to the gallery where he was standing. The spot between her eyes flared red hot.

"What is that?" She ran toward it to get a better look.

Painted on the ceiling beside the well was a large patch of dark blue. Scattered across its wide expanse were golden six-pointed stars with a crescent moon on one side and a sun on the other. In the middle, dividing the moon and the sun was a giant hand extending from a web-like structure that was painted red and black. Vesta stared at it.

Sandor walked up beside her. "I don't know if this is what

you were looking for, but that's definitely related to alchemy," he said.

She jerked her head toward him. "How?"

"Yep," he said pointing toward the painting. "It's the whole idea of their highest goal. Man, that's the hand, reaching for the Divine, represented by the moon and sun."

"I'm confused. I thought alchemy was about figuring out how to turn lead into gold."

"It was, or is. But as above, so below means that they are trying to achieve divinity too. They want gold but they also want the ultimate connection with their creator."

At that moment a white mist clouded over Vesta's vision of the hand and star field obscuring her view. Someone whispered into her left ear in a faint voice.

"The Red King," the warbling voice said.

"What about him?" Vesta asked.

"He knows," the voice trailed off.

"He knows what?" Vesta flicked her flashlight to the left. She swatted in front of her eyes trying to remove the mist which quickly dissipated. No one was there, and the voice was gone. She scanned the gallery but saw only Sandor standing still on her right side.

"Did you have InSight?" he asked.

"Not quite. But I heard a voice say the Red King. He knows."

"The Red King," Sandor repeated.

"It's Javier. He's the Red King." Vesta looked up at the painting. "And he knows all about alchemy." She turned to Sandor. "This was what I was supposed to find."

Vesta began walking back the way they came. "I have to go to that Balenciaga show tomorrow. Javier and maybe Grace know more than they told us. They either were involved in his kidnapping or they know how to find him. I have to figure out which one."

"We," Sandor said as he caught up with her. "We have to figure out what's going on."

Vesta cut her eyes toward him. She knew that she didn't need him to find Peter and, in fact, he would only slow her down. Of course, she couldn't say that to him, he would never accept it. But she would come up with a solution. Her gaze shifted back to the crypt floor as they made their way to the exterior door.

By six o'clock the next morning Vesta was awake and eager to contact Javier. It was too early to call him and decided to wait until nine. For at least an hour she had lain in bed coaxing her InSight to connect her with Peter. Nothing but a black wall came into view. She tried demanding that it show him, yet her vision remained a dark solid mass. Testing to see if her gift was working at all, she focused on Amara and Jared. Their images filtered through the blackness until she saw them clearly in focus walking out of the Broadway production of The Lion King. Their entertainment tastes were so different from hers, but at least she knew her InSight was working somewhat.

Next she tried Liam and found him on a plane. He was sitting in between two beautiful young women, one who appeared to have glitter scattered lightly on her afro hair and ebony skin, the other a pale redhead wearing a bright green catsuit. They were all drinking champagne. She smiled. That was more her style.

Vesta sat up in bed and reached for her running shoes but Sandor had another idea. With his head still lying on the pillow he stroked her back between her shoulder blades. He knew it was a secret spot where tension hid. And that when his fingers gave it just the right amount of pressure, she would stop all movement.

"I need to go for a run," she said as her back muscles began to relax.

"You have plenty of time. Breakfast isn't served until eight-thirty around here. Not even coffee," he said as he moved his hand to her belly and gently pulled her toward him. "Besides, I have something for you."

With his other hand he pulled a fresh red rose from under her pillow. He grasped the long stem avoiding the thorns and traced the rose along the curve of her breast. She smiled, and a sigh floated from her lips as her head leaned back.

"So, the hour or two last night wasn't enough for you," she said.

"I was just getting warmed up."

Vesta turned to look at Sandor and flipped the fluffy duvet off his body.

"Now that you mention it," she said. "You do look hot."

Sandor smiled and pulled her on top of him. "I love you madly," he said.

"You are crazy. There's no doubt."

Falling asleep after sex in the morning was unusual for her, but Vesta fell into a deep sleep for an hour. She dreamed of Peter. He was crying and begging to return to his cathedral. No details of his location came to her. Darkness surrounded him as he huddled in a corner.

"Vesta, I would rather die than stay here," he said.

"No!" Vesta screamed and sat up in bed.

"What's wrong?" Sandor said as his head bolted from the pillow.

"It was Peter, in my dream. He wants to die if he can't return here."

"Could you see where he was?"

"A dark place. That's all I could see. It wasn't my InSight. Just a dream, but I know he was calling out to me."

"Well," Sandor said standing up. "Let's go find him."

Two cups of café crème and a bite from a baguette was all Vesta could force down once they were at breakfast. Sandor on the other hand ate both wedges of brie and ramboulet cheese along with the remainder of the baguette, smoked ham slices, orange juice and two cups of black coffee. She watched him with growing irritation. How could he eat so much? Her nervous energy made her want to run down the rue du Cheval Blanc in front of Le Parvis to the river Eure and back, ten times. Instead she held it inside and watched the minutes on the clock tick by until exactly nine.

She reached for her cell phone lying on the table and dialed the number Javier had given her the night before.

"Javier," she said into the phone. "It's Vesta." She paused. "Yes, it's good to speak to you too. I would like to take you up on your offer of attending the Balenciaga show today."

Sandor pointed to himself. She ignored him.

"It's at Les Invalides at one?"

Sandor poked Vesta with his finger and pointed at himself again. She scowled.

"Yes, that's great."

He raised his eyebrows as he stared at her.

"And please save Sandor a seat too. Yes, that's great. We will see you then."

She hung up the phone. "Don't interrupt me when I'm on an important call."

"Don't try to cut me out of the deal."

"You're in. Did you hear me ask for a seat for you too?"

"Good."

Vesta stood up.

"Where are you going now?"

"To the cathedral of course. I'm going to see if that woman from yesterday is there, the one who gave me the clue."

"Our train leaves at noon."

"I know."

Vesta walked across the cobblestone street waving at the statues of the royals and priests like they were old friends as she entered the cathedral. Since it was Wednesday the massive space was quiet except for the occasional squeak of the wooden door opening on the western entrance. Still wrapped in the dim morning light the nave and aisles lay in idle slumber, rows of chairs stretched across the labyrinth like chains across her heart. Vesta winced as she looked at it.

"Why do they have to cover it?" she mumbled to herself.

A group of Japanese tourists walked past her. They pointed to the rose window perched high on the western wall, their voices excited. She wanted to tell them to return later in the day when the windows would have the sun streaming through bringing the cathedral to life with a kaleidoscope of color, but chances were they wouldn't understand. Besides, they were caught in the trance of the place, anyway. No need for her to interfere.

After walking down the nave to the altar, turning left, and then angling to the right to walk around the apse she headed down the south aisle. She paused in front of the zodiac window and clock again. The British woman in the sensible gray clothing was nowhere in sight. Parishioners began to file in through the squeaky door. It was always easy to tell who they were because they walked directly to a chair near the transept and sat down. They never gawked at the windows or had cameras strung around their necks. They ignored the hordes of tourists and went about their business of being good Catholics.

Vesta continued walking down the aisle. The sound of a door opening and closing on the far side of the cathedral that she now recognized as the office of the priests caught her attention. Mass would begin soon. Enid didn't raise her with any religious affiliation. Rather than Sunday services inside a building, she took her into the fields of summer wildflowers, up the mountain paths by the tiny glaciers and down to the lake by their home on Sundays. There she would talk about being grateful to the Creator of All Things.

"And it's not just these beautiful trees and flowers that surround us but everything," she would say.

"Not the poisonous snakes though," Vesta recalled saying one day when she was a child.

"Oh, yes! The venomous snakes too. They have a place in this world and a reason to be here. They care for their babies just like I care for you. And the venom that comes from their fangs provides relief to people who suffer from arthritis. Did you know that?"

Vesta shook her head.

"Yes, we are grateful for those snakes too."

A knot rose in Vesta's belly when she recalled the memory. Guilt still gnawed at her for not spending more time with her mother. She gazed around the cathedral as it welcomed more sunlight with each passing minute. Enid would have adored the place.

The priest began speaking in his French monotone. Vesta walked further from the transept. No signs or clues from Peter emerged on her walk. She knew the next step was to speak again with Javier and Grace, but she wasn't ready to leave her beloved cathedral yet. And several hours remained before it was time to catch the train.

She stepped inside the store which had opened a few minutes earlier. An older woman sat behind the cash register. Vesta browsed through the refrigerator magnets, pencils, and book markers lined up on the display cabinet in the middle of the tiny shop. Along the wall were books in different languages —French, English and German, mainly. One of the books caught her eye. On its cover was a photograph of the black wooden Madonna and child sculpture from the crypt.

A tingling rushed through her, and her third eye began its familiar spin as her eyes roamed over the background of the photo. Behind Mary and the baby Jesus was the funky hand-loomed-looking tapestry stretched out. Such an odd thing to have in a crypt. She grabbed the book and thumbed through the pages to find more information. Her eyes settled on another photograph of the Virgin and her child. Beneath the image it said she was called *Black Madonna Sous Terre*, or Madonna Under Earth.

"As above, so below," Vesta murmured.

"Pardon?" the woman behind the counter said.

"Oh, no. I was speaking to myself. But I would like to purchase this book," she said as she reached for a credit card in her wallet.

Vesta walked out of the store and over to a chair that was doing its part in imprisoning the labyrinth. She sat down and continued to read about the sculpture. It had replaced one that had been there for centuries but had burned. There was no mention of exactly who put it there or when. Scant information accompanied the photo. She thumbed through the other pages as her breathing deepened. They held more photos of the small chapels in the crypt including the mysterious one next to the *Black Madonna Sous Terre* which contained the arched stained-glass window with the seven steps leading up to it. Her analytical mind kicked into gear. It made no sense to have steps leading up to the window. Once at the top of the steps there was nowhere to go but back down. There wasn't a door, so why have steps leading to it?

The buzzing bee between her eyebrows sped up as she stared at the image. Her next breath brought a psychic lightning bolt striking with a blinding flash. There was an entry on the window but not one that a person could physically walk through. The center of it was different from the surrounding jagged pieces of brown, green, blue, and clear glass that jutted into each other. As she examined the photo, she realized the middle of the window looked like a passageway. Framed by black metal, long pieces of dark brown glass on the outer perimeter of the window symbolically protected the lighter brown rectangles of glass. Moving toward the center visually the earth colors gave way to shades of blue and finally to clear glass in the very center. Jagged pieces of red glass punctuated the exact middle at the top and bottom of the window.

"It's like that weird tapestry, but not," Vesta murmured to herself. "But it's an alchemical symbol for sure."

"You're catching on quick."

Vesta jolted in her chair. "Sandor, why do you do that?"

"What?" Sandor said as he peered over her shoulder. "I was complimenting you."

"I meant for not letting me know you were here."

"You were deep in thought," he said as he walked around the chair and sat down beside her. "And yeah, that's another alchemy symbol."

"It is, isn't it?" She touched the page tracing the doorway in the window with her finger. "That's why the steps are there. Moving from the Earth to heaven. And the red, or *rubedo*, there in the very center at the top and bottom. That means achieving the highest success in alchemy, right?"

"Yep."

"Who made this window?"

"I have no idea."

"The book doesn't say."

"Even if it did, it would be wrong probably. Those alchemists were secretive. Even if they did create this window to leave a clue, they wouldn't broadcast it."

"And it's next to the Black Madonna of the Underground which is more of that as above, so below line of thought. That has to be on purpose, right?"

"I'm sure."

"But why did they build it?"

"I told you, I don't know. You were the architect of this place." Sandor waved his hand at the photo on the page. "But this window was made a long time later."

"I wish I could remember." Vesta pressed her lips together.

"Hey, you did a great job with that spell in your last life to knock your memory out." Sandor shook his head. "You may never get a reboot."

Vesta exhaled and drummed her fingers on the page.

"But you do remember that we need to catch the noon train to Paris?" Sandor pushed the cuff of his Christian Dior shirt sleeve back to look at his Piaget watch.

"Yes, of course."

"Well, it's eleven-thirty."

"Already?" Vesta closed the book and stood up. "I need to change. I didn't bring anything by Balenciaga." She shrugged. "I had no idea we would be going to the show. But I will make do."

"I'm sure you will."

Few things in life are finer than a spring afternoon in Paris when the weather cooperates. Red tulips at their peak grouped in splendid masses along the walkway to the enormous tent on the grounds of Les Invalides. After she and Sandor checked in at the reception table, Vesta walked through the door of the tent dressed in a white Chanel blazer with a white silk blouse underneath and hip-hugging wide-legged black trousers. Her bleached pixie-cut hair was topped by a black Chanel beret.

"Best dressed girl here, as usual," Sandor said as he followed her to their front row seats. "But why did you were that ugly-ass necklace?"

"Because I promised Liam I would." She spoke over her shoulder to him. "And some things trump even fashion."

"Well, tuck it under your blouse. It looks like it came from the Carrefour around the corner."

Vesta frowned, but she had to agree. Her fingers found the necklace as she walked and slid the oddly shaped stones with the dangling crescent moon undercover.

She turned to the left as they reached the runway. Two chairs sat empty, one on each side of Grace Garcia. Her stepson Alejandro slumped next to her in a chair with Javier on the other side. The King of Pentacles stood up and greeted Vesta with quick kisses on both cheeks and a firm handshake for Sandor.

"I am so glad you could make it!"

"Thank you for getting excellent seats for us on such short notice," Vesta said.

"It was no problem because Luciana and her friend wanted to leave early for Italy, anyway." He motioned toward the chairs beside Grace. "Please have a seat."

Sandor greeted Grace with the requisite double cheek kiss and sat to the right of her. He leaned over to the man on the other side of him, shook his hand and began a conversation. Javier stepped over and joined them.

"Ah, I see Sandor has already made friends," Grace said to Vesta.

"It looks like they know each other already. Could be one of his clients."

"It's good to see you again."

"Yes, you too," Vesta said as she shook Grace's hand and turned on her best intuitive radar to scan Grace for anything that would signal whether she was going to try to help or hurt Peter.

"Vesta, have you met Alejandro?" Grace nodded toward the

dark-haired gangly teenager sitting next to her who was staring straight ahead at the runway stage.

"Yes, very briefly at La Bernardin last weekend." She extended her hand to him. Alejandro glanced toward her. His dark eyes framed by his thick black-rimmed glasses, black curly hair and alabaster complexion were a stunning combination. His expression dissolved any handsomeness as he stared, unblinking and wordless at her as he had that night at the restaurant.

Vesta could tell Grace felt the awkward silence. "Alejandro, do you recall meeting Ms. Beauvais?"

"Yes," he said then turned back toward the runway.

Grace gave a little smile. "Well, he's not much for speaking sometimes."

"That's okay. I was hoping to get to know you a little better." Vesta locked her gaze on Grace. Dressed in solid white, Grace wore Balenciaga pants, a white blouse and a jacket. Her white Laboutin pumps revealed the only other color, bright red, on her soles.

"Laboutin makes the most comfortable high-heeled shoes," Vesta said trying to find a way into a casual conversation.

"They are my favorites."

Vesta looked down at her pants. "I wore Chanel today because I didn't know I would be coming to a Balenciaga show while I was here."

"I adore what Karl has done with the house."

"I do too. And I noticed you were wearing his trousers and a turtleneck last night."

"I prefer his designs to Nicolas, but Javier being so closely tied to the house..." Grace's sentence trailed off.

"Sure. I understand that." Vesta commanded herself to be hyper-alert as she watched Grace's face for any clues. "So, have you ever been to the cathedral at Chartres?"

"Once when I was a girl. I remember it as a magnificent place. My mother took me to see the windows. My governess and I walked beneath them. She told me about the bible stories depicted. I wanted to join my mother in the crypt but I was told she was there on business matters so I wasn't allowed." Grace looked down at her hands then up at Vesta. "I love feeling like I'm surrounded by the Earth. All the things to be learned by being in nature."

A tingle rushed up Vesta's spine. "Why was your mother in the crypt?" she asked leaning forward but trying not to seem too interested.

Grace shrugged and shook her head. "I don't know."

Vesta relaxed a bit and leaned back in her chair. She noticed Grace had no tension in her face or body. Her manner felt straight forward and honest. Vesta caught herself. But she could be really good at pretending. As she searched for something to keep the conversation going, she leaned forward again.

"My mother loved nature too." She nodded. "And she always dressed in white."

"Really?"

"Yes, we lived on the side of a mountain in Colorado. We were always gathering herbs and things she found in the forest to make medicines for people who would come to see her."

A light brightened in Grace's eyes. "She was a healer!"

"Yeah, she was."

"Are you?"

"Absolutely not!" Vesta held her hand up. "I never wanted anything to do with it. She never made any money. She wouldn't accept it." Vesta shook her head. "She never understood the value of having money. It always seemed pointless to her."

"I understand how she must have felt." She looked down at her hands. Diamonds glittered from each ring finger and a diamond encrusted Rolex laid on her wrist. She smiled. "I know how ridiculous that sounds, but I wouldn't care if I had no money at all. It's Javier..." again her voice trailed off.

"I guess if your grandmother could turn lead into gold then you never really had to worry." Vesta smiled.

"She never accomplished that. I believe my grandfather did though."

Vesta lowered her chin and stared at Grace. "You really believe that?"

"Oh, yes. It's all there in his papers." She leaned forward in her chair. "You see, he committed his life to it. His talent as an artist was put to painting about alchemical subjects such as *Le Vaisseau du Grand Oeuvre*. And his talent as a writer of books was put to writing about the same. He was consumed by it."

"But he turned lead into gold?"

"He and my grandmother worked with many chemical substances, crystals and stones. Their formulas were very detailed going from the *nigredo*, to the *albedo*, to finally the *rubedo*."

"The *rubedo* was the final step, right? And *rubedo* means red."

"Yes, but it's much more complicated than that. Ultimately they were trying to connect with God."

"I've heard that was part of it too. As above, so below."

Grace smiled. "I see you know quite a bit about the ancient art."

"Not really. Only the little bits that I've picked up over the past few days. I don't understand the whole connection to God thing."

Grace nodded. "Yes, it can be confusing. Alchemy came into being over a thousand years ago from the Arab region. The word 'Al' in Arabic means the Supreme Being, as in Al-lah. Alchemy is known as the science of God, or the chemistry of Al.

It is the art of perfecting nature and the generation of inanimate and living substances."

"Okay." Vesta cocked her head. "That is some intense stuff."

"It is. Before he died, my grandfather, in his laboratory notes, promised to write down the formula that finally worked."

"Did he?"

"I don't know. I have never fully researched his library. Only some journals he kept." Grace patted Alejandro on the shoulder. "Although Allie has."

The teenager turned his head and glared at her as he shrugged off her hand. "My name is Alejandro. You two would do well to stop talking about something you know nothing about. Besides, we are here for the clothes right now."

Vesta raised her eyebrows.

"Forgive him," Grace said. "He speaks without a filter. It has always been his way."

"Yeah, in America, we call that rude."

An apologetic smile slid across Grace's face and she nodded. Vesta's gaze moved in for a closer look at Alejandro. The shiny black velvet jacket and matching pants were undoubtedly Jean Paul Gaultier from the previous fall collection. A singular masterpiece from the designer. She reached across Grace and touched his arm.

"Alejandro," Vesta said.

He instinctively jerked his arm away but turned his head to look at her.

"Your Gaultier suit is beautiful."

His piercing dark eyes and locked jaw softened for a second. The compliment had clearly caught him off guard. Yet, a moment later the cold brooding mask slid back into place. Vesta knew she had found a crack and wanted to prise it open further. "I especially loved when Tanel Bedrossiantz wore it last fall on the runway."

This time Alejandro's eyes lit up without hesitation like black obsidian glittering in bright light.

"Did you see the show? My favorite was the black cape with the red roses that he wore." His fingers made excited movements as he spoke. "I was sitting behind Grace Coddington and I could tell she loved it the most, too."

Alejandro's gaze flicked from Vesta to a space somewhere above her head. The spark in his eyes extinguished as fast as if a bucket of sand had been thrown on the flame. Dull pools of mud replaced the shine. Vesta turned her head to see Javier standing above her to her right.

"Alejandro, get up," he said. "You have a better seat than our honored guest."

"Oh no!" Vesta said. "I'm fine here. He doesn't need to move."

Javier kept his gaze on Alejandro. "Of course, he does."

The boy stood up. Vesta did too. She knew it was a power play for all to see and she was being manipulated for Javier's benefit. But she had no choice at that moment. As she switched places with Alejandro, she smiled at him but he ignored her. Javier walked to the next seat and sat down beside her.

"You have a much better view now."

"I'm still on the front row," Vesta said hoping she sounded polite but sarcastic.

"The show was scheduled to start already," he said. "But you understand how these things go."

"I've never been to a fashion show that started on time. I would be shocked if one ever did."

"I'm happy you understand."

"It gives you and I some time to discuss the disappearance of Peter."

"I'm afraid I told you everything I know."

"You said you met Peter once. Can you tell me when that was?"

"It was a performance of Mozart concertos in the cathedral about a year ago."

The spot between Vesta's eyebrows began to twitch. It wasn't the usual spin or burn, but almost a tickle. With a brush of her finger against the patch of skin she acknowledged the sign.

"Can you tell me more about that concert?"

Javier eyed her. She could feel his gaze trying to penetrate her thoughts. No way would she allow that to happen.

"The acoustics were acceptable," he replied in an off-hand way. "Maybe more than acceptable. A grand piano was moved to the transept."

"Excuse me, but I meant could you elaborate about your conversation with Peter."

"There was very little, actually. I introduced myself because of course I had read of Peter in my personal diary."

"Are you referring to the one that you keep from lifetime to lifetime bringing you up to speed about who is in the trionfi?"

"Certainly."

"And you had read about him, but never met him before? Even though you live part-time in Paris and he's just an hour away?" Vesta pressed on with her line of logic.

"The ancient saint who walks at the cathedral was never part of my business which frequently takes me around the world."

He paused and waved to someone who walked past them.

"He offered to give me a tour of the place," he continued.

"Did you take him up on the offer?"

His eyes turned back to her and watched her closely.

"I did."

"Did you walk the labyrinth?"

"No. It was closed for the evening. But he showed me the stunning windows. It was a pity that I couldn't see them in all their glory during the day. I'm sure they are magnificent."

"They are." Vesta could feel her pulse quicken but she commanded herself to allow no change to be apparent on her face or body even though her third eye began to spin faster.

"Did you visit the crypt?"

"Well, yes. It is the largest one of all the medieval gothic cathedrals in France."

"Did you find anything of interest down there?"

Javier paused again and studied Vesta's face.

"I feel as though you are wanting to ask me something, but are either afraid to or don't know how to ask it."

"I'm not afraid of anything," Vesta said with a relaxed, unblinking expression on her face.

"That's good. So, please, what is your question?"

In Vesta's mind she knew it would be pointless to flat out ask him if he knew where Peter was. If he did, he would lie. If he didn't, he would say he didn't and she wouldn't be sure if she should believe him or not. She grazed her third eye again with her finger because the spin had turned into an irritating itch. Over the past several months, she had come to recognize when that happened it was trying to convey concealed information to her. She clenched her jaw. Its message wasn't coming through. She was failing at her job. The only course of action called for would be to continue with her logical analysis and push on until she got what she needed.

Her intuition told her that Grace knew nothing about Peter's disappearance. The woman's manner was too open and easy as she responded without hesitation to her questions. In fact, neither Grace nor Javier had presented themselves as anything but cooperative. Maybe Javier was trying to help her after all. She wished she could get a firm reading on him but her intuitive compass wasn't cooperating. But he had been inside the Chartres crypt and he did know a lot about alchemy.

"Did you see any signs of alchemists down there?"

Javier let out a small laugh. "The practitioners, no. Their symbology? Yes, many places in the crypt."

His penetrating gaze dove deep into her. "Do you know about the alchemical work in the crypt?"

"I'm learning about it. And I discovered quite a bit there."

"Well, that's not the place to look for alchemists. At least not at this time of the year. And not for your friend."

"What do you mean?"

"Have you ever heard of the Paneveggio Forest?"

"No."

"I think you might find Saint Peter in that place."

"Why?"

"Because on the twenty-first of May each year a special ritual is held there, the secret night chant of the Stradivarius tree."

"That's tomorrow. The secret chant of what?"

"It is very remote, this forest. A perfect place to hide someone. Keep them out of view. If he has been kidnapped as you say, then that is a good place to look for someone who would do such a thing."

The lights in the tent dimmed. Underneath her skin the little energy vortex between her eyebrows lit up like a blowtorch, a signal that vital knowledge had been acquired. She would pounce on it immediately.

"Have you told Sandor about this?"

"No."

"Don't tell him." Vesta paused. "Let me."

"As you wish, your Highness." Javier smiled.

A rhythmic Euro-style beat began to waft from giant speakers placed around the room. Models dressed in black with black leather bands wrapped around their heads stepped out on the runway and pranced toward her. Vesta could barely keep her eyes on the fashion because her brain was sorting through the information Javier had just dumped on her. What was this ritual and secret night chant in the forest all about? Why would someone take Peter there? He could be anywhere. Except Chartres. He wasn't in Chartres.

Then a thought crossed Vesta's mind that caused her to jolt in her seat. She controlled her body movement, so it was just a minor knee jerk, but her brain was buzzing. Javier said it was a ritual. What if the kidnappers were going to sacrifice him? The image of the Tower card popped into her mind. She could feel sweat bead up on the back of her neck. Don't overreact, she silently demanded. She didn't know that as fact. But the thought began spinning around in her head. Did some crazy alchemist grab Peter and take him to the secret forest? Vesta pursed her lips. There was only one way to find out.

Chapter Seven

The Balenciaga show concluded with Nicolas Ghesquière walking out briefly to wave at the crowd who applauded with great admiration. Everyone stood up after he left the stage and began mingling together in little groups.

"Couldn't he come up with some other color besides black?" Sandor whispered in Vesta's ear when he walked up beside her.

"There was some white. Weren't you paying attention?" Vesta said. "I thought it was a beautiful show."

"I'm ready for a drink. You?"

Vesta paused. "Um, yes. That sounds great. Perfect." She didn't like lying to him, but it was necessary. "There should be a bar set up somewhere close by. Want to go find it? I'll wait here."

"I'm on it," Sandor said as he took Vesta's hand and gave it a quick kiss before heading off toward the crowd filtering out of the tent.

Vesta turned toward Javier who was in conversation with two gentlemen. He cut a glance toward her, made a brief comment to them, shook their hands, and turned to face Vesta.

"The show was spectacular. Yes? Nicolas honors the Basque heritage. Cristóbal would be proud."

"I'm sure you're right." Vesta blurted out the words as fast as she could. "Javier, this forest you mentioned. Tell me again why you think Peter would be there."

"Because it occurs to me that whoever stole your saint is not your average thief. He is not after jewels or money, because my assumption is that Peter has neither."

"You're correct."

"So, one can only conclude that he wants something more, how should I say, esoteric." Javier leaned his head to one side as if considering the subject. "For such people the ritual at the Paneveggio forest holds great allure."

"And this happens on May twenty-first?"

"Always."

"And how do you know about it?"

"From the journals in Grace's private library that I have browsed through on occasion."

"That is when they say the trees are ready to be harvested to obtain the best wood for the violins."

"Like the Stradivarius violins. That's what you meant?"

Javier nodded.

"But I don't understand what that has to do with a ritual."

A smile crept across Javier's face as he eyed her.

"If you should be interested in knowing more, I can provide you with the information."

"I do want more. If there's a good chance that I can find Peter, that's where I need to go."

"The tree cutting is mundane for the men with their saws and instrument makers choosing their trees during the day. But there is magic in the forest on that night and the alchemists are aware of it."

It was a solid lead dealing directly with the crazy group that had taken center stage in her search for Peter. And she could check it out right away to confirm if it had any validity.

"Okay. What airport do I fly into?"

Javier shook his head. "It is deep in the Dolomites. You must take the train. The town closest to the place in the forest is called San Martino di Castrozza."

Vesta studied Javier's face. His dark eyes showed no emotion. And his face with the well-manicured mustache and closely cropped beard held no tension in his jaw or forehead. Could he be right? Was Peter being held in a cabin in a forest for some bizarre ritual? If she went there, she might find him or she might not. But if she didn't find him, she could return to Chartres and begin her search in a new direction. At least she would have ruled out the May twenty-first event because she was there and found out for herself. Maybe that was why the King of Pentacles appeared in the spread with Peter and the Tower. Perhaps it was telling her that Javier would help her locate Peter by suggesting the Paneveggio forest.

She blinked and smiled at Javier. "Thanks for your help. I need to go. I have a train to catch."

Javier nodded and smiled. As Vesta turned, she felt a hand take hers.

"I enjoyed our conversation," Grace said.

"I did too," Vesta said hurriedly as she looked her way. "I apologize but now I'm in a rush. Javier thinks Peter may be held in the Paneveggio forest in Italy. There for a ritual tomorrow night. I have to go. And it sounds like it's going to take a while to get there."

Grace frowned. "The night the forest sings?"

Vesta stopped and stared at Grace. "You know about it too?"

"Yes, my grandparents were there on that night."

"It sounds like a good lead, so I'm going." Vesta waved to Grace as she walked toward the exit.

"Whoa! Where are you going in such a rush?"

"Oh, Sandor." Vesta knew she didn't want him tagging along with her. He would slow her down and try to put in too many of his own thoughts and suggestions which more often than not wasn't what she wanted to do. She didn't have time to argue with him about what to do next. The best thing for Sandor would be a little diversion. But he was smart, so she would have to be smarter.

"Here's your champagne." He handed her a glass.

"Thank you." She held the glass not daring to drink it. "So, did you find out anything from Javier?"

"Nothing that will help us find Peter. He and I both know one of the head managers of the Rothschild hedge fund. That was the guy we were talking to. But I got zero on any leads. I think we should talk to some of the priests at the cathedral. Maybe they saw something."

"Well, I was given a couple of ideas that I think we should explore separately to save time before we return to Chartres." Vesta gave Sandor one of the most-sincere smiles that she had ever mustered.

"From who?"

"Actually, Javier and Grace. Javier mentioned the catacombs as a good place to look. And Grace said Sacré-Cœur basilica had a crypt that was closed to the public but could be a great hiding place."

"Why separately?"

"Because I don't want to waste any time." She handed her glass to Sandor then turned to leave.

"Hey! Don't you want your champagne?"

The pale gold liquid looked inviting and delightful but she knew that even a few sips would take her intuitive radar off course. It was one of the sacrifices she knew she had to make to be at the top of her game.

"No, they're both for you."

"Wait a minute," Sandor said, his dark eyebrows furrowed deep. "You want me to head from here into those moldy catacombs way out by Montparnasse? And you're going in the opposite direction up to Sacré-Cœur?"

"Yes."

"The catacombs are one of the biggest tourist sites in Paris. You can't hide somebody there."

"Apparently there are restricted passages. Check those out. You're the Magician. You got us into the crypt last night. You can do this."

"This doesn't sound like a well-thought-out plan. What do I do if I find him?"

Vesta's eyes widened. "Call the cops, of course." Vesta turned away from Sandor. "And I'll do the same. We can meet at Le Parvis later, or the cathedral," she said over her shoulder.

As she walked out onto the sidewalk in the bright afternoon sunlight to hail a cab, Vesta realized she felt guilty about lying so demonstrably to Sandor. But she had no choice. He would come up with too many questions and delays. Time was crucial to her. If anything slowed her down, she might not make it to the Paneveggio forest by tomorrow.

Inside the cab she laid out her plan. First, she would see if she could fly faster than take the train all the way to Italy. But she must go to Chartres to pack clothes for two days and get her passport. From there she would either head to an airport or take the train. Along the way she would find a bookstore to learn as much as she could about the forest.

The train for Venice departed at four o'clock from Chartres. Never had she moved so quickly and with such precision once she arrived at Le Parvis throwing her dressier clothing out onto the bed leaving only casual pieces in her luggage. She ran down the creaky spiral staircase and out of the door. With only two minutes to spare Vesta stood on platform B of the little station watching the train pull up. She hoisted her bag up the steps and along the narrow aisle to her seat in first class. One of the best tips she had learned early on in travel was to pay extra for first class. Especially on trains. Coach cars were always crowded and noisy. But true to form, this car was empty.

Javier had been correct. Even though she could fly to Venice from Paris, it would take longer according to the plane schedules than to take the train. From there she would need to rent a car to drive two and a half hours to San Martino di Castrozza. As the train pulled away from the station, she fished the ragged copy of Fodor's *The Best of Italy* out of her handbag. When she saw the book lying on the small bookshelf in the dining room as she flew through the door of Le Parvis she grabbed it with the promise to William she would return it. But as she turned it over in her hands looking at the curled corners of the pages with the numerous coffee cup rings on the cover, she decided a sparkling new copy was in order for the hotel.

Daylight drifted over the edge of the world and an inky night flooded the landscape as the train approached Lyon four hours later. The stop was quick—to unload and load a small crowd of travelers. Vesta closed the book and laid it in her lap. She took a mild interest in the people going and coming from the train as she gazed out the window. An older Asian man joined her in the first-class car. His tall, wiry frame reminded her of the character Ichabod Crane from *The Legend of Sleepy Hollow*. The expensive-looking cane he walked with added to her appraisal. While it was straight enough, the cane had several knot holes bumping out of the surface along its length. The high polish of the wood and the curious nub of a flame on the handle caught her attention. He sat down in a seat on the other side of the aisle two rows ahead of her.

The train lurched forward in a gentle manner calling her

attention back to the platform as it pulled away from Gare de la Part-Dieu. Vesta removed her shoes. It would be another eight hours before they arrived in Venice. Grenoble and Turin would be quick stops that, with any luck, Vesta would sleep through. Rest had become essential to her for recharging her psychic battery. Massaging her neck, she recalled the years of sleep deprivation she endured while in college. The days in class and the nights at clubs. It had been a consequence that she dealt with for years. There was too much to accomplish back then, and she had managed it all, plus her studies and various jobs at bars and restaurants.

She leaned back on the headrest. Sandor would have returned to Chartres by now. He would have found her note explaining that she received InSight to go to a forest in northern Italy to find Peter. No cell phone service was available, so it was impossible for her to call him at this point. He would be angry. She was certain of that, but he had insisted on coming with her even though she told him that there was no need.

Time meant everything in the rescue of Peter. Lengthy discussions about the best way to approach the situation weren't an option. The plan was to go into the forest, to the place described in the travel book, and launch a thorough search for him using her most finely tuned intuition during the day when the trees were being cut and during the night when the alchemists were supposed to be there. Of course, the travel guide didn't mention the nighttime ritual. That was a secret according to Javier.

The forest was quite large so she would logically figure out the best way to canvas it. If she didn't locate him, she would leave, regroup in Chartres with Sandor and lay out a new plan. If she did find him, then she would do whatever was necessary to help him escape his captors. A call to the police was an option, but she didn't want to get them involved unless she knew he was there. Years of living in New York City before her luxury apartment and the constant cab rides had taught her how to think on her feet. More than once she had faced, and narrowly missed, getting mugged, robbed and raped. She knew how to read people, especially when their energy was malevolent. It didn't take being the High Priestess of the tarot to figure that out.

Minutes passed, and she fidgeted. Sleep wouldn't come no matter what she tried. A glance out the window only gave her a reflection of herself in the glass with the endless blackness of the night as a backdrop outside. Closing her eyes did nothing. Her thoughts kept revolving around Peter. Where exactly was he? For months her InSight had been razor-sharp bringing whatever she focused on into her mind. Now it was as dull as a plastic picnic knife at the bottom of a beer cooler where he was concerned. Someone or something had blocked it to prevent her from seeing him. Luc's music had broken it down, but that wasn't available at the moment. She needed to slip into her dream world where she saw Peter the night before. It wasn't the same as her InSight but was a connection that would offer some help.

Vesta drummed her fingers on the book while chewing on her lower lip. A remedy did exist, but she didn't want to go that route.

More minutes crawled by. Meditation had never been easy for her even though she thought she had mastered it in the past few months. But now, any attempt to clear her mind only caused more thoughts to jump in. Relentless thoughts about how she needed to stop thinking. Self-critical thoughts about being a failure at not thinking. Thoughts of not being worthy to hold the position of High Priestess.

Vesta slammed her hand down on the book causing the old man two rows ahead of her to turn his head and look. She shot him a quick grin and raised her right hand to signal that everything was okay. Before another thought came to the surface, she stood up. When she boarded the train at Chartres, she noticed the dining area a few cars away. Maybe it was still open. What she was about to do wasn't her first choice or second, she told herself, but now it seemed to be her only choice.

She pulled francs from her purse, got up and walked past Ichabod Crane. Even though the train was probably at its full speed of close to three hundred kilometers per hour, the ride was smooth with only a gentle swaying side-to-side as it sped along the tracks. Passengers in the next two cars were either asleep or busy on their laptops as she passed by them. Inside the third car she found the kiosk for food and beverages. A plump woman with gray hair askew in a bun got up from her chair behind the counter.

"Hello, what do you have to drink?" Vesta spoke in English before she considered that the woman might only speak French.

"Here," the woman said as she pointed to an array of bottled water and carbonated drinks lining the wall behind her.

Vesta pressed her lips together and exhaled. "No." She paused. "I meant wine. *Avez-vous du vin rouge?*"

The woman nodded. From under the counter she pulled a bottle of Bordeaux with its cork halfway out.

Vesta looked at it a moment then nodded. "Okay." As she placed twenty francs on the counter and watched the woman pour a glass full of the dark red liquid her pulse quickened. A spark of adrenaline raced up her spine. The voices in her head—in her heart—began arguing. She needed sleep to tap into her subconscious mind to hopefully see Peter, as well as the rest it would provide for the day ahead, one said. But she had promised herself she wouldn't drink alcohol when she was on official High Priestess duty, the other protested. It was a character flaw, a weakness, that she must overcome. It didn't help with her InSight, it only made her energetic field feel like Swiss cheese.

The woman slid the glass of wine toward her. Vesta left the twenty-franc bill on the counter and walked away even though the woman was saying in French that she had change coming. A wave of her hand signaled to the woman that everything was good as Vesta made her way past the sleeping travelers and the computer zombies back to her car. Even Ichabod appeared to be asleep, his head cocked at an angle against the headrest, as she walked past him. Her ears popped indicating a pressure change. They must be going up a mountainside as they approached the Alps.

Vesta slid into her seat. She pulled the tray down and set the glass of wine on it. An exhale pushed past her lips as she stared at the glass. A year earlier she would have drunk an entire bottle of wine by now. And never had a second thought about it. But now she knew too much. It wasn't just the fact that she was one of the highest-ranking members of a group dedicated to protecting the planet and its inhabitants. It was owning up to the truth that she had used alcohol for decades to mask her relationship issues. From the guilt she felt over her mother, the conflicted feelings she had about her father and sister, to her inability to let another human get emotionally close to her, she made martinis and glasses of wine her buffer.

It was also the truth that a part of her still enjoyed those drinks, still enjoyed the separation of herself from the others, the anesthetizing of her emotions. Things were easier that way. But everything changed when Uncle Raymond died. The pain and shock struck her as hard as Enid's passing. A chasm opened up somewhere deep inside her pulling all her tears and rage and love inside. She could feel it still. Wine helped her fill that empty space.

She picked up the glass and ran her thumb along the side.

Not feeling anything had gotten her through those horrible times. It allowed her to climb to the top of Sybarite and turn it into a first-class clothing and luxury goods company. Alcohol numbed her to anyone else's feelings so she could focus on her goals and achieve them. Her success had been trumpeted in business journals and women's magazines. Young women admired her and rivals were riddled with envy. Men wanted to take her to expensive dinners and exotic locations. Everyone wanted to be close to her because she didn't want to be close to anyone.

Vesta laughed in a half-hearted way that only those who know a deep, painful truth can laugh. The train car swayed, and she looked out the window into the abyss of the night. Her reflection looked back at her. The face of a woman defeated in spirit, looking every bit her forty years. She felt her blood cool to an icy temperature as she lifted her chin. The mission was to find Peter, and she wasn't going to accomplish that if she wallowed in self-pity.

"That was pathetic," she said to her reflection as she picked up the glass and drank its contents dry. She set it down and leaned her head back. Six hours of sleep would be enough for her to feel ready to go in the morning.

Chapter Eight

When the mind relaxes its grip on thoughts, so many thoughts, it can wander into uncharted realms, for better or worse. Vesta found herself in such an unknown place. She was walking through one of the meadows near her childhood home in Crested Butte, Colorado. The sun shone soft and bright as birds chirped with vigor in the tall pine trees. An abundant mixture of wildflowers and grass brushed her knees with every step she took. Turning the corner by the giant boulder that had rolled to a rest from the mountain top eons earlier, she saw her mother, Enid, and her Uncle Raymond sitting on a fallen log. They were young, as they must have looked when they were children.

"Mother? Uncle Raymond? What are you doing here?"

"Waiting for you, of course," Enid said.

"Am I dreaming?"

"I suppose you could call it that," Uncle Raymond said.

Vesta shook her head. "I don't understand. But I'm glad to see you both."

"Your heart knows what's true. That's all that matters." Enid stood up and walked toward to Vesta. She reached out her arms. Vesta bent down and hugged the child, her mother. Love flooded through her limbs, her stomach, her head and her heart. She didn't realize how much she had missed her mother's hug until she felt it again. Fragile arms, so stick thin they could snap at any moment, yet strong with a binding energy that surrounded her, radiated from her.

"Ah," Vesta said as she melted into the embrace.

"I feel it too," Enid said.

"Uncle, I didn't forget about you." Vesta loosened her grip on her mother and embraced Raymond. Then she sat down on the log looking at them both.

"Well, I know enough now, all of us being these living tarot card people life after life, to not be freaked out by this, but still." Vesta paused. "Am I dreaming?"

Raymond patted Vesta's hand. "It's not a dream in the technical sense of the word."

"Then how else can it be that you're both children?"

"That's how we like to be when we're not confined to physical bodies," Enid said.

Vesta raised her eyebrows, nodding slowly. "Okay."

"We communicate with each other, as well as you and the other trionfi, when you're in the theta brainwave state," Raymond said. "It's quite an elegant method, really. But it does require some practice on the body's part to get into it. That's why we asked Li Wei to help us with this shortcut."

"Who?"

Raymond looked down at his little legs as he wiggled his barefoot toes.

"Our physical forms are encumbrances after so many lifetimes, but they are necessary to do our jobs."

"Yes, my job!" Vesta stood up. "I have to find Peter." She froze for a moment staring at Raymond. "Do you know where he is?"

Raymond smiled. "On an energetic level, yes. We always know where each trionfi member is when we're in non-physical form. Geographically on the planet? Not really."

"I have to find him before someone kills him. And my InSight has stopped working."

"That is why we arranged this," Enid said.

"Arrange this dream, or whatever it is, to help me find Peter?"

"To help you find yourself." Enid took Vesta's hand. "Let's sit down here."

The little girl sat next to the log in the tall green grass dotted with coreopsis and Indian paintbrush. A rustling sound behind Vesta caused her to turn and see a mountain lion loping in a slow gait toward them.

"Oh my God!" she screamed.

"No, it's alright," Enid said. "That's my spirit animal. She likes to be near me."

"Your what? You're saying it's tame?"

The mountain lion walked up to Enid and rubbed its enormous head against the little girl almost toppling her to the side. She laughed as the cat then lay down beside her and began purring.

"She's more than tame," Enid said. "Stroke her fur. You'll see what I mean."

Vesta released her held breath with a gush. "No, I don't need to do that. I'm fine."

"All of what you see around us is our psychic rendering," Raymond said. "We created the environment we desire. No more, no less."

"But let's focus on why we contacted you," Enid said.

"To help me find Peter."

Enid smiled. "To help you. And then, in due course, you will find Peter." She stroked the head of the content lion by her side as she spoke. "Your InSight hasn't failed you, but it has been blocked."

"There is a tremendous build-up of energy on this side of the veil," Raymond said. "We are here to guide you on how to release it."

"It's necessary for the natural balance that it be released," Enid said.

"You see," Raymond continued. "When I was in my physical form this previous time, I was able to equalize the energy without your assistance. Now I can't make such adjustments in the physical plane as I'm still too young."

"Wait," Vesta said. "You're still too young? Does that mean you're alive again? Reincarnated?"

"We both are," Enid said. "I was fairly certain you knew that I had returned to the physical world from the theta experience you had in the bathtub on Valentina's island. Do you remember?"

Vesta looked down at the rich earth under her feet and nodded slowly. Enid had come to her, as a child that day, and spoke to her about how to build an impenetrable wall around her mind so that no one could read her thoughts.

"I remember. I hadn't really thought about it much since, but I do remember that dream, or whatever." She looked up. "Where do you live? Can I come see you?"

Enid smiled. "No. That could create a treacherous time space overlap that causes severe problems sometimes."

"Are you brother and sister again?"

Enid looked at Raymond and beamed a radiant smile. "Yes."

"And you already know who you are? I mean in regards to the trionfi?"

"Enid certainly does, but I'm a newborn. Today is my birthday."

Vesta stared at Raymond trying to form words. "Your birthday?" She managed to say. "As in, you were born today?"

"That's right. Our parents are thrilled."

"Are they trionfi too?"

"Oh, no. But they will be loving to us and that is all that matters," Enid said.

"My dear, we have strayed off our intended path, and this energy dissipates after a time, needing to recharge in a cosmic sense, you understand, so we must hurry now."

"Yes, please understand that your InSight hasn't disappeared. You must trust yourself to remove the blocks that have been set before you."

Vesta noticed that she could see the log behind her uncle's legs and the lion appeared to be fading into the tall grass.

"Call upon the knowledge that lies buried deep inside you. Your spell didn't abolish it. You can recall it," Raymond said as his body now was an outline of what it was before.

"It is vital that you recall your power, you alone must do it, not so much for Peter, he doesn't care if he lives or dies, as long as he is in his cathedral, but for the world. There is much for you to do."

Enid had faded to a dull, opaque form and was splintering into tiny star-like fragments.

"Use your intuition, don't doubt it. It will never fail you." Her last words came not from her mouth but from the grass, flowers and trees as they too disappeared into an all-consuming cloud of blankness.

The essence of Vesta floated in the white nothing, or was she part of the nothing? She wasn't sure. Had she been in this place for eternity or only a second? A bolt of lightning rocked her senses back to life. She could see the bright yellow, hear screeching, taste metal, smell ozone and feel an electrical charge careen through every cell. Out of the ghostly void an image came into focus. Something familiar. Peering intensely at it she realized it was her own face very close up.

Zig-zagging toward her, another jagged arrow of lightning hit, this time above her left eyebrow carving a deep paper-thin cut. Instead of blood oozing out, a tiny yellow figure with a head, two arms and two legs wiggled out of the gash, climbed onto her brow and sat down. Vesta stared at it as it stared back at her. Then it crossed one leg over the other and began swinging it impatiently. It seemed to be waiting on her to do something.

"What? What do you want?" She asked without actually saying any words.

It gave no response except to cross its arms and continue to stare.

There did exist a part of her somewhere—was it her brain or something more expansive—that knew what the little yellow creature was and what it was waiting for. She wanted it too, but she had to find the key first.

Vesta became aware of a heaviness and felt her head rocking back and forth. Her eyes slid open to see the train as it was rattling to a stop in a station. A sign strode by her window that read Venezia. She blinked several times willing herself to become fully alert from what felt like a sleep of a hundred years.

She had arrived in Venice. The empty wine glass still sat on the fold-down tray in front of her as she raised her head off the seat headrest. She was stunned that one glass of wine could make her sleep so solidly for six hours. Or was it solid? An awareness inched closer to her. It had something to do with her mother and uncle. And a tiny yellow person? It lay on the periphery of her conscious mind but wouldn't come closer. Vesta shook her head. There was no time to think about it now because she needed to focus on unloading her bag and finding the car rental place. And procure a cup, or two, of Italian espresso.

The old Asian man who looked like Ichabod Crane with the polished, crooked cane was dragging his bag in halting motions from its perch over his seat. Vesta plunked her bag onto the floor and rolled it to the exit. She hurried back into the train car.

"Let me get this for you, sir." She rolled his bag to the exit then pulled it off the train onto the platform, then followed with her own. The wiry man stroked his pointed chin as he stepped off the train.

"Thank you. You are most kind, Miss."

"Just call me Vesta."

"Vesta. Thank you," he said as he turned to leave. "I'm Li Wei."

As she was pulling her bag away in the opposite direction, she heard his last words and hesitated. His name, she recognized it from somewhere before. What about it was she trying to remember? There was something important, but she couldn't quite latch onto it. Make a mental note to remember what it is later, she instructed herself. First though, she needed to get a car.

Leaving Venice, like leaving Paris, was never easy. Memories of checking into the Gritti Palace, having a massage in the spa then cocktails on the terrace she treasured. Plus, the city filled with its beauty and mystery called to her like a siren, but she stayed focused on her mission.

Two and a half hours was the approximate time it would take to drive to San Martino di Castrozza according to the guy who rented the car. Enough time to lay out a plan in her search for Peter. According to William's ragged book, the Paneveggio forest spans two hundred square kilometers. Any attempt to cover such a vast area alone in an efficient amount of time would be futile. Rather than relying on her intellectual strengths of strategy and reasoning, she knew that her trionfi gift of intuitive guidance was called for. But since her InSight was blocked regarding Peter, she would have to let her less powerful third eye be the divining rod once she was in the forest.

As the thought crossed her mind, the previous night's dream flashed like a neon sign in her brain. She had been with her mother and uncle. The recollection of being in a meadow close to her childhood home bloomed into full color throughout her conscious awareness. Her pulse quickened so much that she felt her cheeks flush not only because she realized she had a conversation with them but because she could actually recall their embraces. Vesta closed her eyes and smiled as she paused at a stop sign. A sense of happiness and well-being spread through her. How she missed them and the unconditional love they gave her.

The smile on her face dissolved when she thought about what they were saying. Enid and Raymond told her that her High Priestess intuition hadn't disappeared, and she alone had the power to clear the path. Trust her intuition, they said. Uncle Raymond told her to call upon her knowledge which wasn't lost but rather buried deep inside.

That would be part of her plan. She would take their advice calling upon her latent knowledge buried deep in her psyche when she cast the spell on herself at the end of her previous life. Pieces of her intuitive power had already come back when Amara began schooling her on the basics of her gift. She remembered how to recognize and control the activation of her third eye, her InSight, when it would pick up on what needed her attention. How to use the Waite-Smith tarot deck for divination also returned quickly. Even the best tarot readers were no match for her when she laid out her three-card spread. Her High Priestess super-power of seeing the future, unless altered by concerted effort of free will, had already helped Jared and Cyrus shut down both large-scale white-collar and blue-collar crimes. A sense of pride welled up inside. Something blocked her intuitive capabilities. It was time to find out what, clear it out and reclaim what was her gift and duty.

Any anxiety she felt melted away as she drove from Venice into the northern Italian province of Tretino. The landscape morphed from marshy flatlands to pine forests and the jagged peaks of the Dolomites. Once ancient coral beds lying in a shallow primordial sea, the chalk-colored mountains seemed determined to rip apart the sky above them. Vesta's thoughts swam around what the Earth must have been like when the oceans were so high that these majestic peaks were under water. A time before humans, but was it a time before the Elders visited?

Vesta pressed her lips together. Not much information had been shared about who the Elders were, or still are. Where did they come from? And how were they able to give Vesta and the other trionfi their special gifts. At some point she would ask Amara about it. If anyone would know more details, it would be her. That question would have to be explored later. First came Peter. Her InSight remained lost in an ethereal fog, dense and unyielding. No sight, no sound of him. But she would change that soon.

Caught in a continuous stream of thought, Vesta was surprised when she realized that the town of San Martino di Castrozza lay directly in front of her. Turning left off the main road she saw the Hotel Regina on her right. While the other buildings in the little town were constructed in the ski chalet style, the Regina stood out with its bold semi-circular shape and solid white stucco walls. It reminded her more of a lodge at Euro Disney than a serious shelter for her rescue mission. Of course, there was a part of her who liked the kitschy style and was glad they had a room available at the last minute.

After checking in, freshening up and changing her clothes into a pair of Calvin Klein khakis, a lightweight white sweater, and a pair of Nike sneakers, Vesta headed to the hotel's dining room for lunch. The hostess guided her to a table outside on the terrace under the sunshine and vivid blue sky. While eating her green salad accompanied by a small hunk of local-made tosella cheese and freshly baked bread, she examined the map she obtained from the front desk. Paneveggio forest was gigantic. Time to be patient for a few minutes and let her intuition set a course.

She looked up from the map and sipped her sparkling water. The effervescent liquid satisfied her desire for something else that tingled on her tongue besides champagne. A long slow exhale slid out of her mouth as she let her eyes wander about the scene, giving her mind a chance to connect to her inner guide.

Activity had increased on the street in front of the hotel. A few families walked past her speaking in Italian, a language she had never taken the time to learn and quite different from French. The tone of their voices was jovial and the cotton bags stuffed with food and bottles of wine gave Vesta the impression they were headed into the forest for picnics. There were also small groups of men who called out to each other across the street. Most carried backpacks and seemed to be in a hurry.

The waiter walked up to her table. "Madam, may I get you something else?"

"No, I'll take the check." She pointed to the bustling street scene. "But can you tell me what's going on? All these people. Is it because of cutting the trees?"

"Ah, yes," he said. "Many people come for this every year. They enjoy meals in the forest and watch as the men decide which trees they desire. It is very pleasant."

"I see. Thank you."

The waiter handed Vesta the check and returned inside the restaurant. She was pulling lira from her pants pocket when she heard a voice behind her.

"Excuse me."

Vesta turned her head to see a woman, probably in her fifties with soft brown hair, an easy smile and brown eyes that could only be described as wise.

"I hope I'm not being too personal, but are you here for the Song of the Forest too?"

"Um," Vesta hesitated. "I am. I heard about it from a friend."

"It's quite remarkable. I've attended a few times before." The woman stretched out her hand. "I'm Angeles. Angeles Arrien."

Vesta picked up no sinister energy, only something that resembled a vibrational hug. She put her hand out accepting the handshake.

"Vesta Beauvais. Are you a musician?"

"No. I'm a cultural anthropologist."

"Oh. Are you doing research?"

Angeles nodded. "And you?"

Again, Vesta hesitated. "I was um." She hated stumbling for words. The mark of a bad liar. "Hoping to reconnect with a friend who might be here."

"Well, I hope you do."

Vesta laid the lira on the table and stood up. "Thank you. And I hope your research goes well."

Angeles smiled. "It was good to meet you Vesta."

As she turned to walk into the restaurant, she caught a glimpse of a tall, lanky figure clad in solid black walking across the street. A mop of brown hair obscured most of his face. He entered a shop and disappeared behind the door. Vesta froze, staring at it. Out of the millions of people in the world whom she had seen either live or on television or the movies, only one moved like that. Liam was in town.

It must be a mistake, she thought as she rushed through the

dining room and out the hotel door. Why would Liam be in San Martino di Castrozza? It didn't matter, she had to catch up to him. Two steps into the street her peripheral vision caught sight of a car zooming toward her. A man standing several steps behind her yelled something she didn't understand as she jumped back toward him, stumbling but regaining her balance. The car sped past her without slowing down.

"Senora!" the man said.

"I'm alright," she said smoothing her hair behind her ears.

"Okay?" he asked.

"Yes, thank you."

"*Pazzo*," he said shaking his fist at the car. "Crazy."

"Yeah," Vesta said as she looked both ways for moving cars before walking out into the street again. Successfully on the other side she stepped up to the shop where she saw the man wearing black disappear. Inside was a gallery. Paintings of flowers, photographs of the mountains and wooden bird and fish sculpture filled the space.

"*Buon giorno*," a petite man with a long gray ponytail greeted her.

"Hello. I saw my friend walk in here a minute ago. A man dressed in black, tall."

The man cocked his head.

"*Le chemise noir*." She pointed to her shirt. "I don't know how to say it in Italian."

"In here?" he asked.

Vesta nodded. The man furrowed his eyebrows and looked around.

"No. Not here."

A quick scan of the room verified what he said. Liam was clearly not in the room. Vesta scratched her head.

"I was sure that was him," she mumbled to herself. "Okay," she said to the man. "Thank you. *Grazie*."

Vesta left the gallery but stood by the door. She was certain she saw a man dressed in black walk through the door, whether it was Liam or not she couldn't swear but where did he go? The car nearly hitting her had taken her senses off center a bit but she saw him before that. Vesta shook her head. In the old days, which meant last year, she would have headed straight for the bar, any bar, to have a cocktail and settle her nerves. Part of her wanted to do that now, but she wouldn't. It was almost two o'clock. She needed to get into the forest. Without thinking about it any further, she walked past the gallery toward the chalky mountain range at the end of the road.

Within five minutes she walked up to a visitor's center and something that looked like a petting zoo with young deer wandering around inside an enclosure. The families she saw earlier were clustered nearby sitting at picnic tables eating. Vesta veered away wanting to find a quiet place. A trail marked Sentiero Marcio began at a quaint covered bridge spanning the Travignolo stream. Clear, fast-moving water cascaded over jagged rocks twenty feet below her feet as she crossed the bridge into the forest. Stepping off the well-defined trail she walked deep into the red spruce territory crossing another smaller bridge until at last, the chatter of people was replaced with the gentle whoosh of the wind through the trees.

Every direction she turned the scene was the same. Skyscraping trees creating a permanent shade for the healthy green moss covering the ground. Vesta inhaled. Fresh pine scent mixed with dampened earth. She closed her eyes and smiled. It reminded her of the forests around her childhood home. Her intuition told her it was time to stop walking. A large rock fairly flat on the surface looked to be a perfect spot to sit. She hoisted herself up, coming to rest about three feet off the ground.

The breeze rustled through the trees but otherwise a deep quiet surrounded her. Another solid inhale and exhale brought her awareness inside. Enid and Raymond implored her in the dream, or whatever it was, to trust herself to revive her InSight of Peter, to remove the block. How did the block get there? Maybe she was doing something wrong in accessing it. It had worked easily before, but suddenly just stopped. Again, her intuition nudged at her. It wasn't anything she did. Someone had blocked it as it regarded the Hanged Man of the tarot. Otherwise it was fine.

Vesta fingered the necklace Liam had given her. It had become like a part of her own body now that she wore it all the time. The oddly shaped stones with the silver crescent moon dangling down brought her comfort in some strange way. Perhaps that wasn't Liam walking into the gallery after all. What would he be doing out in the middle of an Italian forest?

"Focus, Vesta, focus," she murmured. Her thoughts, as usual, jumped like rabbits from one subject to the next. Calming them, slowing them down was essential now so that she could let the subtle energy of her intuition take over. She inhaled long and slow then let it slip out with ease. The tingling of her third eye began. A welcome sensation because it meant she was tuning in beyond her conscious reality.

"Where is Peter?" she whispered to whomever in the non-physical realm might be listening.

Body awareness drifted away. She closed her eyes. Her breathing remained deep and steady. From her mind's eye the Paneveggio forest spread out beneath her as though she were looking at it from high above. Hyperawareness filled her with the sense that she was part of the forest, seeing and feeling the movement of each needle stirred by the breeze. It was a sublime feeling where every tiny motion sent her into a state of ecstasy.

"Ah," she sighed and hoped for more.

To the far right of her field of view a small clearing appeared. Bright green moss in what looked like a perfect circle covered the floor as glowing orbs of light danced above it. The scene filled her with joy for some reason completely unknown to her. That was the place she needed to be, there was no doubt.

A snapping sound, perhaps a small pine branch, brought her awareness back to the rock on which she sat. She opened her eyes to see a giant buck deer standing in front of her. Even sitting three feet off the ground, the animal still towered above her. His antlers spread wider than her arms could outstretch. His large brown eyes stared at her. Then he spoke.

"I apologize. I didn't mean to disturb you."

Vesta's mouth dropped open, but no words came out.

"I could tell you were one with the forest, but I wanted to offer my help."

"You wanted... you can... talk?"

"It's really a mental telepathy-type arrangement. You might realize that my lips aren't moving."

Vesta hadn't noticed because the fact the deer was speaking to her had consumed all her attention. But as the words continued to come from him, she did note that his mouth stayed motionless.

"But how?"

"Animals communicate this way. Humans used to be capable of it too, but most of them lost it many generations ago."

Vesta responded with a nod.

"When you entered that state of transcendence, when you merged with the forest, I knew you would be able to hear me. Your mother told me this would happen."

"My mother?"

"Yes, she's the one who sent me."

"Why?"

"To make sure you find the spot in the forest tonight where it sings."

Vesta's eyes lit up. "Do you mean the little clearing in that direction?" She pointed to the right. "Where the little orbs of light were dancing around?"

The buck nodded his majestic head. "Then you saw it."

"I did. Is it far from here?"

"Follow the path until you see the tree with a crown at its base. There you turn right. Listen carefully and walk toward the sound of the flowing water."

The deer began walking away.

"Do you know if Peter is there?"

"I do not."

"Can I communicate with all animals now?"

"If you like."

"Okay." Vesta searched for something else to say. "Thank you."

The deer walked away without further response. Vesta blew out a huge exhale.

"Wow. That was a trip."

She looked at her watch. It was four-thirty. By the time she walked back to the hotel, showered and changed clothes it would be time to leave. One quick motion vaulted her off the rock and squarely on the ground. Four small chalky rocks, a landmark she had made a mental note of was to her left. Next would be two pine saplings in front of a much older tree with a large knothole at the height of her head. Enid had taught her how to create landmarks for walks in the forests at home. The memory of her mother claiming to know each tree and animal as an individual popped back into her mind. When she was a child, she first embraced the idea but later as an adult thought it was preposterous. Today, after talking to a deer telepathically, she believed her mother's assertion without question.

A sad smile rippled across her face as she thought about how her mother had such patience and love for her despite the knowledge that her daughter had willfully cast a spell on herself to forget who she really was in this life. Of course, she also knew the reason why the spell was cast. The memory of trying to protect her mother but making a poor choice and causing her death was the final weight dropped on her soul that took its tragic toll. The other trionfi had variously mentioned that they too had moments, incidents in their previous lives that tested them, rocked them, and slashed at the core of who they were. It was completely understandable, she thought, when life after life is a reincarnation as the same person with the same job. And around the same general group of people.

Someday soon she would like ask each of the trionfi for their own stories of how they coped with such devastating times. Especially Liam since Sandor had already shared his harrowing story of the life before this one. And Peter, poor, dear Peter. She kept walking and returned her attention to navigating out of the forest. The two saplings were straight ahead. Go on the left side of them keeping the sun at her back for about a thousand yards. The little bridge would be to her right and she should hear the fast-moving water before that.

As she walked a tingling of her third eye accompanied by a prickly sensation on the back of her neck began to take hold. In her short experience of recognizing intuitive signs, she understood that combination meant danger was close by. She scanned the forest around her. No animals or people were visible. Everything was still and quiet except for the rushing water that she could hear ahead. The small wooden bridge came into sight. She was almost back to the main trail.

A bird, the first she had heard in the forest, let loose a shrill cacophony of notes. Between her eyebrows the spot on her forehead grew hot. Was the bird a threat to her? Her intuitive radar was definitely signaling that something wasn't right.

"I'm not going to run," she whispered to herself. "But I am going to walk fast."

Vesta stepped quickly onto the bridge. She could see the clear water below her crashing on the sharp-edged dolomite boulders turning its spray a brilliant white. The boards were damp but not slippery. Midway across the span she heard a loud crack and felt the wooden plank beneath her give way. Her right foot slipped past the broken piece into mid-air as her left foot skidded on the wet board ahead trying to stay put. Another loud cracking noise echoed in her ears as she felt that plank also break in two. Panic raced through her mind and body. Every cell screamed and fired inside her. Both feet had the unfathomable feeling of absolutely nothing underneath them.

"No!" she bellowed like a thunderclap.

Her right hand grabbed for and trapped the bridge's railing in her grasp. It was slippery but she willed her hand to hold fast. She swung her left hand over and took hold of the railing digging her nails into the wood. Her legs dangled above the jagged rocks and rushing water below. With every ounce of energy in her body she pulled herself up enough so she could bend her right knee and swing her leg up to the next plank on the bridge. She listened for another cracking noise but it didn't come. Pressing more weight onto the plank she hoisted herself up on the bridge.

A throbbing pain shot from her right foot up through her body. Blood trickled from a gash on her ankle. Afraid to stay on the bridge any longer than necessary, Vesta stood up then limped the rest of the way across to the bank. Sweat beads ran into her eyes. When she wiped them away, she noticed her hand was trembling.

"Stop it!" she shouted to herself. "Stop shaking!"

She pressed her lips together hard and her right hand made a fist.

"Focus. And breathe," she commanded.

One breath in for the count of four, hold it for four, let it out to the count of four. After five repetitions of the pattern the trembling was gone, the perspiration stopped, and she was breathing normally.

She knew she had to start walking on her swelling ankle or the muscles would stiffen making it hurt worse. By her calculations, it was a twenty-minute walk to her hotel. A sharp pain raced up her calf as she put pressure on it. It was manageable though. Trying not to limp was more of a challenge but one she could also manage. Careful not to slide on the damp moss, Vesta walked to edge of the bank where a puddle of clear water stood. She dipped her hand into it then washed the blood from her ankle. The cut wasn't very deep. A ragged piece of the plank probably scratched her when her foot fell through or when she swung it back up. Either way, she would be fine.

The next landmark back to the main trail was a fallen spruce with its top pointing due north. From that place she veered left to head directly to the designated path.

As she walked, she thought about the fall and what lead up to it. She realized that the bird could have been warning her rather than making a threat. It sounded logical after all.

"Why not?" she argued with herself. "A deer was talking to me."

Aside from almost falling to her death on the rocks below, which would have surely happened if she hadn't pulled herself up, her journey into the Paneveggio forest had been successful. Trusting that she hadn't lost her intuition allowed her to see the clearing in the forest where she needed to go. It maybe also allowed her to open up to the telepathic message from the deer. The one her mother sent.

Vesta slowly shook her head. Not only did she believe Enid sent the deer, but she believed Enid had already reincarnated and was alive again. A chill ran up her spine. Two worlds crashing together, her life as CEO and chairman of the board of

Sybarite and her recurring life as the High Priestess of the trionfi. Family members dying and reincarnating in some unknown location and having the power as children, even a newborn, to come to her in a dream, or whatever that was, to offer advice.

"I need to up my game," she said out loud.

If they could do that at such a young age, she needed to regain her InSight and do her part in this crazy family tree. The fallen red spruce was in view on her right. She veered left. Random bits of chatter began to filter through the forest, children's laughter and a chainsaw buzzing through a tree. Soon she would be back on the main trail.

Questions remained in her mind about the bridge. It seemed fine when she walked across it the first time. No cracking noises. Nothing to indicate there was anything unstable. Maybe she put her foot on just the right place, the weakest spot, to make it give way. She would tell someone at the visitor's center at the trailhead about it.

The rest of her trip to the hotel held no unexpected events. For that she was grateful. Inside her room she slipped off her clothes and slipped into a hot bath. She thought about her old habit of having a Russian vodka martini while soaking. One, ice cold with a fresh wisp of lemon rind perched on the rim, would be perfect at that moment to help her relax.

"Ah," she cooed at the thought. But she would not allow it even though something tiny but vicious gnawed at her somewhere inside to relent. Shame filled her senses. As the High Priestess she should be above such cravings. The moment she realized who she really was, the urge for a glass of wine or a cocktail should have disappeared. But they didn't. It was a constant struggle.

Enough of soaking in her own pity. She commanded her thoughts to shift to Peter. Was he near the clearing that she saw in her vision? That had to be the reason she tuned into it. A slight ping stirred between her eyes. To her that meant yes. Her heart beat faster. The plan would be to follow her intuition, and the directions the deer gave her. Deep inside she knew that whatever happened she would be able to handle it. On her forehead her third eye spun like a loose wheel rolling downhill. It was a good sign.

Chapter Nine

Dressed in black Donna Karan slacks and a black turtleneck with the idea that blending into the night-time landscape might be best, Vesta left the hotel at seven o'clock. The sun had set behind the mountains casting a rich darkness everywhere except for the dazzling sky above which blazed with the light of the Milky Way. The waning crescent moon wasn't visible yet and wouldn't show its sad face for at least an hour. Following the instructions of the giant buck deer, she guided herself past the visitor's center onto the Sentiero Marcio trail. She turned on her flashlight, grateful that Enid had taught her as a child to always pack one when traveling. About two miles along the trail, she began to wonder if she had missed her mark when her tiny spotlight caught the image of what looked exactly like a crown made of wood at the base of a large red spruce.

Three triangles with a tiny knothole crowning each sat on top of a rectangle protruding from the base of the tree. It was all part of the tree and had grown organically but it looked like a crown had petrified into wood. Vesta stared at it, amazed by the intricacy and perfection. She had found her landmark and from this point she turned right to go off the trail. The only other thing to do was listen for and head in the direction of running water.

Everything was silent in the forest. How was she supposed to know which way to walk when there were no sounds of water?

"Listen carefully." She heard the voice of the deer echo in her mind.

Vesta stood still and closed her eyes. One deep breath in and all the way out vaporized her thick coating of ego. She let the essence of the forest draw near her, inside of her. An ecstatic pause engulfed every cell as she waited in anticipation for the next moment. And she realized the forest wasn't quiet at all. The trees were vibrating in harmony with one another, a sound so gentle yet dynamic. In front of her, behind her, on each side they reverberated. As she listened, she could pick out individual notes. They were singing! And the song was more beautiful than anything she had ever heard.

"Ah!" she gasped. Tears trickled down her cheeks as her body expressed the emotion felt by her soul, and mind, and heart.

In the distance she could hear the sound of flowing water. She opened her eyes and walked toward it. The forest sang to her along the way. No distinct words, at least not in any language she could understand, instead sounds were linked together that resonated deep within her creating a sublime harmony, a psychic alignment. This must be what Javier meant by the secret night chant of the forest.

"Magic happens in these woods," she murmured to herself. And each step confirmed it.

The song grew louder as she walked further into the forest until it was almost deafening in her ears. The notes called attention to different parts of her body. First her tail bone, next the area below her navel, then her navel itself which caused her to imagine the sun bursting from her belly into the sky. A vibration around her heart began after that creating the sensation of unconditional love coming from her toward everything and everyone in the world—in the universe. Following that she felt the need to speak, to say words carefully chosen, impeccable of the way she felt. The truth as she knew it. But no one was listening, she thought, before she caught herself and realized, everything was listening. Her third eye began to spin. And rather than the hot spot on her forehead that she had grown accustomed to, this time it felt like a giant drop of water flowing out of her forehead into the cosmos to blend with an ocean of other drops. It became absorbed by the infinite and she could see the infinite as the top of her head felt like it spread wide open.

Her feet were carrying her through the forest but they weren't making a sound. Vesta was light, not substance. She moved through the trees as what the old-timers in Crested Butte would claim to be a fairy. What they would see on moonless nights when their campfires were doused but before they fell asleep.

It was in that state that she floated from the forest into a clearing. She recognized the perfect moss-covered circle she had seen in her vision earlier in the day. Inside this fairy ring were other orbs of light, just like her, dancing to the rhythm of the night chant. Human forms swayed and pranced inside each giant ball of light. No one spoke, yet each greeted the others with a telepathic symbol that Vesta could see in her mind's eye of two snakes intertwined around a long pole like the medical caduceus symbol with two crowns stacked on top of the pole. One looked exactly like the crown that had been her landmark. She tried to hold that symbol in her thoughts, hoping she was conveying that as a mutual greeting. Whether she did or not didn't seem to matter to the others as their ecstasy captivated them. Three more orbs of light joined the group so that, as best Vesta could count, twenty-four total were now in the mossy clearing.

The singing increased not so much in volume but in the vibration within her body. Seven distinct centers from her sacrum to the crown of her head resonated to the notes. Physical sensation merged with something greater like a psychic tuning fork. Her cellular make-up, her DNA, appeared to dissolve into and become part of the pulse of the universe. Awareness of this connection catapulted her into a higher vibration. She could feel the other light beings around her drawing closer. Together they formed a circle that began to spin. Vesta saw the fairy clearing they were in, but she saw more.

Images, memories, transparent yet fully visible to her, flashed in rapid succession. The first was her in her Sybarite office looking out the windows onto Manhattan. Next came the labyrinth in Chartres with her dressed in a long black cloak and hood standing in the center. That image faded into an outdoor scene of tall grass and a lively spring that she, dressed in a white gown, was bending over. The last was set in the nighttime where a huge fire was blazing as several people, including her, stood around it. They were dancing and chanting to a deep rhythm. As they swayed and dipped around the fire, three human-like figures approached. Each was over seven feet tall with long, graceful limbs and large, dark eyes. Vesta felt a great outpouring of love for them even though she had no idea who they were.

The spinning of the circle increased as Vesta lost the images in her mind. A vortex of light and sound enveloped her, spinning but standing still at the same time. Was the event horizon of a black hole like this, some part of her wondered. The feeling of being ripped apart, without any pain, surged through what she thought, more than likely, was her body. In the next moment everything stopped. The light and chanting vanished. She became hyperaware of being in her body which felt like a shoe two sizes too small.

Looking down, she wiggled her fingers and toes as though she was getting acquainted with them for the first time. Strange little things, she mused. But necessary. Voices began murmuring around her. Human voices. She looked up. Women and men stood in the large circle that she was part of. A few spoke to the person next to them. Sighs and light laughter wafted across the moss-covered clearing. Her eyes traveled around the circle. Young faces, older faces weathered but beautiful, happy faces, and... Liam.

Vesta's eyes flicked wide open. "Liam!"

He looked across the circle and smiled at her. She took a step to approach him but found her balance off kilter.

"Wait," he said. "I'll come to you." He walked, not with his usual nonchalant gait but with a slow, sure step.

"Are you all right?" Vesta asked.

"Oh yeah." He brushed a flap of brown hair from his eyes. "It's just that after one of those alchemy prom dances you have to start back in these heavy meat suits a little slowly."

He leaned in and gave her a big hug.

"Alchemy prom dance?"

Liam laughed. "Well, that's what I call them."

"What just happened? And why are you here?"

"Ah, yes, this all rather needs an explanation doesn't it?"

Vesta raised her eyebrows as she nodded.

"Let's take a stroll, to get our physical bearings back into good working order, shall we?"

Liam wrapped his arm around Vesta's shoulder. They began meandering around the clearing. Other people were walking too, probably for the same reason. Smiling faces said quiet hellos as they passed.

"You see, aside from being a part of the everlasting trionfi, I'm also an alchemist. A high ranking one, at that. And you stumbled upon this place on the very night the forest sings. We in the alchemy world learned how to transfer that energy into the hedonistic spectacle you joined. I'm guessing your gifts as High Priestess allowed you to tune in."

"I didn't stumble upon it," she said. "I made a special trip here to find Peter. Javier said whoever kidnapped him would probably bring him here."

"In the circle?"

"He didn't mention the circle. He said the forest. Do you know if he's here?"

"I haven't seen him."

"Maybe he's in another location in the forest."

"No. He's not." The voice came from behind Vesta. She whirled around to see another familiar face.

"Grace!" Vesta's eyes widened. "What are you doing here?"

Her dark eyes sparkled like two polished pieces of ebony contrasting with her pale skin, white shirt and pants. "We must talk Vesta. I have discovered important information about Peter."

"Were you part of this whole prom dance thing too?"

"No. No. But it was so beautiful to observe. I always love seeing it."

Vesta wrinkled her forehead. "Always? Like you've seen this before?"

"Yes. Many times. My grandfather wrote about it in his diaries. And my grandmother would come every year."

"Who was your grandfather?" Liam asked.

Grace looked at Liam. "Julien Champagne."

"The alchemist and painter of *Le Vaisseau du Grand Oeuvre?*"

Grace smiled and nodded. "I see you know of him."

"That means you're Grace Garcia."

"Oh, I'm sorry," Vesta said. "Yes, and this is Liam Spencer."

"I have known of Mr. Spencer and his wonderful music for a long time."

Liam took Grace's hand and kissed it. "Ever so pleased to meet you."

"And this," Grace said as she motioned to someone standing slightly behind her. "Is my friend Angeles Arrien."

The woman with the eyes of wisdom whom Vesta had spoken to at lunch stepped forward.

"Hello," Angeles said to Liam.

"Greetings," he responded.

"Vesta, this is Angeles."

Angeles smiled in her easy way. "We met this afternoon, at the hotel."

"Good. We are all acquainted," Grace said. "Now I must get to the point of why we came."

"Please do. You said Peter wasn't here," Vesta said.

"That is correct," Grace said. "Can we walk some place nearby for privacy? I know a special place."

"More special than this?" Vesta asked as she looked around at the towering red spruce surrounding the perfect circle of moss.

"It is a place where my grandfather claims in his diaries that he made love to my grandmother for the first time."

"Sounds like a spot I need to see," Liam said.

As the four left the clearing Vesta noticed they seemed to be following the path of the moonlight that had made its way above the mountain peak and carefully snaked its way between the towering trees shining only on the forest floor. Vesta considered mentioning this anomaly but then thought about all the other events that had already transpired that day and decided this was on par. She could hear water splashing on rocks close by. The silver moon-stream wandered through the trees for several yards more, their steps following its trail, until it appeared to dead-end at a huge boulder.

Grace stepped inside it. Vesta blinked her eyes hard. Did she just see that? Did Grace really dissolve into a rock? Grace leaned her head and hand out motioning for the others to follow her. As Vesta drew close, she realized it was an optical illusion. There was actually a narrow path between two boulders of the same size allowing a person to slide through. Vesta followed Grace as they emerged from the slim walkway into a small hollow where a crystal-clear steam gushed from underground. A palpable energy crackled in the air like an early, blue sky morning after a heavy snowfall. Crisp, full of potential. Psychically electric.

"Where's the river or waterfall?" Vesta asked.

"What are you talking about?" Liam said.

"Well, I was told to follow the sound of flowing water once I turned off the main path."

"This is it," Liam said.

"Can't be," Vesta said. "It's too small. There's no way I heard this, two miles away."

"But it is," Grace said as she bent down to let the stream run through her fingers. "You see these waters have to do with the attainment of the highest stage in the spagyric or alchemical phase. The tinctua can occur here because the water is so pure. Only true alchemists and those with a special gift can hear the water from a distance and find the clearing. Ancient magic made it so."

Grace pointed to the mossy bank. "This, according to my grandmother's diary, is where my grandfather first made love to her." She looked up at the group. "And perhaps where my mother was conceived."

"And you, Vesta, I think could hear the water because of your own intuitive abilities as the High Priestess of the tarot," Angeles said.

Vesta whirled around to face Angeles. "You know who I really am?" She turned to Grace. "I didn't think we were supposed to tell anyone."

Angeles smiled. "She didn't tell me. She didn't need to. Your energy spoke for itself." Angeles looked toward Liam. "Just like you, who the cards call The Fool. But by no means are you. That was merely an expedient way for the storytellers long ago to describe someone lacking in fear. So courageous, yet at the same time always striving to achieve a state of ecstasy."

Liam cocked his head. "Hm. That's a good way to describe me. I like it."

"Angeles is well versed in the tarot. She focuses on it from a cultural perspective studying the images created by Lady Harris for the Thoth deck," Grace said. "But don't worry. She would never divulge your identities or the fact that you are actual living people. She is from the Basque region, like Javier, where secrets are guarded forever."

"I'm not worried," Liam said. "And I'm also confident Vesta will find Peter and save him. That's why I put her on the case."

Vesta directed a half-hearted laugh toward him not sure if he knew about the alchemy connection before he contacted her, but something she definitely would ask him later.

"Okay, so now about Peter," Vesta said looking at Grace.

"Yes, he is still in Paris. And it was Javier who had him kidnapped."

Vesta gasped. "How do you know this for sure?"

"I heard him talking in his study yesterday after the Balenciaga show with Alejandro. He figured out the truth and confronted Javier who admitted it. I overheard the conversation from my private library. They didn't know I was there."

"Why? Why would he kidnap him? And from the little bit of InSight I did see, the message from Peter said he was going to be killed."

"I don't know the answer, but I believe I know a way to help you find your sight. Let's return to the clearing and I will show you."

Grace turned to leave the water's edge. A twinge in Vesta's belly echoed her thought earlier that she would be happy to stay at the stream for a while bathing literally and metaphorically in its waters.

"I see your attraction to this place," Angeles said as if reading her thoughts. "This stream is very much tied to your energies of intuition. It's a physical manifestation of energy. In fact, one of the alchemical symbols is a crescent moon, like the one you're wearing."

Vesta looked down at her necklace. She ran her fingers across the silver moon dangling from the chain and the scratched, misshapen beads.

"A special gift from me," Liam said.

"I'm sure it is," Angeles replied.

"We must go. There isn't much time." Grace led them away from the stream and back to the clearing. Sitting on a large rock at the edge of the forest Vesta saw a familiar woman with short black hair wearing a navy hoodie, white button-down shirt, and blue jeans. She was deep in conversation with another young woman.

"Luc!" Vesta and Liam shouted unison.

The woman looked up and smiled. Grace, Angeles, Liam, and Vesta all greeted her with warm hugs.

"Now, Vesta and Liam, please meet Abby," Grace said. "She is Luc's girlfriend who is studying physics at the Sorbonne."

"Pleased to meet you both," Abby said.

"Luc, you didn't tell me you were coming to our little gathering tonight," Liam said.

"Well, I wasn't planning on it but Grace called me. Abby and I were in Venice on holiday. It sounded like an emergency so we came right away."

"It is indeed an emergency. I will explain everything to you but first, did you bring what I asked?"

"Yeah," Luc said as she pulled a Walkman from her hoodie pocket. "Here it is." She handled it to Grace.

"Thank you. I will walk with Vesta back to the stream. Then I will return and tell you everything I know."

"We're going back?" Vesta asked.

"It is vital. Let me tell you why as we walk."

Vesta nodded. She and Grace left the alchemists' circle and the others. They followed the moonlight once again as it made its path through the forest toward the secret place.

"You see," Grace began. "Luc told me about your experience listening to her music. I understand that what she creates is unique. Although I make no pretense to understand exactly what it all means. I do believe, Vesta, that you will benefit from hearing her music again. Perhaps your InSight, as you call it, will return to you. Or at the very least you will be aided again by listening."

"Grace, you asked Luc to bring her chakra music here for me?"

"Yes."

Vesta smiled as tears welled up in her eyes. She knew she could gain her InSight listening to Luc's combination of acoustic science and metaphysics. The fact that Grace thought of it and went to the trouble of arranging to be there, to bring Luc there, was beyond what she could have hoped for.

"Oh my God. That's awesome. You're awesome!"

Inadequate words to express how she felt, but all that she could speak at that moment. Grace paused and turned to face Vesta, the moonlight shining on her pale face turning it ghostly white.

"You must find your Peter," she said. "I'm not sure why Javier captured him, but I do know that when he sets his mind to achieve something, he lets nothing stand in his way."

Chapter Ten

Vesta took the lead as they made their way through the forest and between the giant boulders to the mouth of the stream. She could smell the fresh water yards before they reached it. Even in Crested Butte the streams caused by snow melt never smelled so alive and clean. Drawing in a deep breath she silently instructed the charged molecules to circulate through every cell in her body. On the deepest level of her being she recognized this was the nourishment she had been starving for. Her synapses sparked making her fingers and toes tingle.

"Would you find a place that is comfortable to sit?"

"Yes," Vesta said as she climbed up on a waist-high boulder beside the stream.

Grace handed her the Walkman and a pair of earphones. "Her music is ready for you," she said. "I will join the others. I hope it helps."

Vesta smiled at Grace. "Thank you. I am so grateful for your efforts." Grace nodded then disappeared into the boulder.

Surveying the scene before she closed her eyes, Vesta wanted to sear the perfect image that surrounded in her mind forever. Water gushing from beneath a large rock spilling across a mossy landscape dotted with towering red spruce. A billion stars overhead encapsulated her like a cosmic snow globe but also invited her to release herself to the infinity that beckoned.

One earpiece went into each ear. She took in a deep breath, let it out, and pushed the play button. A hum began, low in tone, reverberating slowly. She closed her eyes. The rock beneath her felt like it was vibrating, but then she realized that the rhythm was coming from inside her. It took hold of her senses anchoring her to the place she sat. A melding of her and the boulder's surface began as an ethereal chord from what she guessed was a keyboard swelled into her awareness. It stayed constant and grounding. Another deep breath came and went unnoticed. The deep resonating sound that reminded her of Amara's squatty brass bowl being thumped by a chubby wooden stick made the muscles in her hips relax. After that, she knew the sounds were changing but her brain wasn't paying attention to the details. Instead, it began drifting into other dimensions.

A brick wall appeared in front of her. It didn't take more than a second for her to sum up the situation.

"So that's why my InSight stopped with Peter."

When she reached out her hand and touched it, she could feel the cold, rough texture. Balling her hand into a fist she pounded on it. Solid, unmoving, it resisted. She pushed on it, but nothing budged. An image of her body appeared in her mind, and with all her strength she ran full force into the wall. No response came, not a brick out of place or even a particle of dust flew into the air. She felt no pain from slamming her imagined body into the wall. Such corporeal things didn't exist where she was at that moment.

Fluttering and a frenzy of many things striking the wall on the other side, like butterfly wings, caught her attention. She could tell they were as desperate in their attempt to get out as she was to get in. Looking at the wall she recalled that every defense can be broken. It was a fact learned early in her business career. Her logic kicked in as she studied the situation. What was the origin of the defense? A memory began to stir. There was another wall that she remembered. One she built to keep others from reading her thoughts. That wall was built from the bottom up, brick by brick, knitted together like a psychic sleeve. A slow nod, maybe from her physical body sitting on the boulder, signaled her adoption of a plan. Weakness had been identified.

The solution was so simple she laughed at herself for taking such a slow approach. She watched herself climb up the wall, finding every crevasse for a foot or hand to gasp onto. In seconds she was on top. She grabbed the last brick laid to keep her away from her InSight to Peter, she pulled it up with both hands feeling it turn loose with a groan. All the bricks were attached to one another with a mortar of energetic magic that followed behind the first brick, disappearing into the ether above her as she flung them out of her way. Steadily, she descended the wall as each layer she stood upon vanished until she was left standing on a flat white surface. Nothing could be seen in any direction except more vast blankness.

Armed with the knowledge that the vicious block had been dissolved, she drew in a cleansing breath and let it out sure and strong. InSight with Peter was hers once again.

"Focus, Vesta. Focus," she murmured knowing it was time to find him.

A blurred image crystalized sharp and clear as she watched. It was her, sitting on the rock as the stream danced in joyful leaps beside her. With her next exhale the vision shifted to a scene of the others standing in the clearing. They were laughing at something Liam had just said. She smiled. The vibration from Luc's music within her was still strong, but the hum had changed into something else. It sounded like the feeling she had when a breeze rustled leaves on a tree on a perfect summer afternoon. More of an experience than a sound, but one that described the music better than anything else could.

Sandor came into view as the scene in the clearing faded. He was in Paris at Harry's New York Bar in the first arrondissement sitting at the bar talking to a beautiful woman while smoking a cigarette. She smiled at that too. There was never any reason to worry about him. Imbued with skills beyond measure as the Magician, Sandor would always make the best out of any circumstance.

The lightness in her heart grew heavy as Sandor's image dimmed and Javier's solidified in her mind's eye. She watched as he sat in a room lined with dark-paneled walls and rows of bookshelves. A rust-colored leather chair squeaked as he leaned forward to examine a book open on the desk. It must be the library that Grace spoke of. He read in silence for a few moments until a hulking man dressed in a dirty gray sweater entered the room.

"Everything is set," the man said. "The priest will be delivered to the tower tomorrow."

"He's not a priest."

"Whatever he is, he'll be there tomorrow."

"Be on time."

The man nodded as he lumbered out the door.

Were they talking about Peter? They had to be. And what tower? Adrenaline flooded Vesta's body. The scene began to wobble in her mind like a television with bad reception.

"No!" she blurted out. "Stay focused."

The image came back together. Javier was thumbing through pages in the book. She needed to know where Peter was going. There were a hundred towers, at least, in Paris. It might not even be Paris. Watching Javier read wouldn't give her what she needed. Shallow breaths started moving her chest in and out in a chaotic spasm.

"Stop it!" she stammered.

Her breathing slowed.

"I want to see it from the beginning." Vesta spoke with slow determination. "Show me from the time Peter was kidnapped. Show me everything I need to know."

Whiteness filled in the space of Javier's library as though a cloud entered it until the room vanished. In its place the quiet beauty of Chartres cathedral chapel of the Black Madonna appeared. Vesta felt herself sigh. Peter stood in front of her and the divine baby as he made the sign of the cross. He turned to leave as Javier approached him.

"Monsieur Peter?" Javier smiled. "I apologize, I don't know your last name."

Peter smiled. "I really don't have one. Peter is fine."

"Ah. I am Javier Garcia. I'm also a member of the trionfi, the head of the house of Pentacles."

"We've met before. The last time was when you asked for my help after that little revolution we had. You wanted to butter up the bishop so you could buy most of *les chateaux* in this area after the owners lost their heads."

Javier looked down at his Ferragamo shoes and nodded. "Yes, my diary from that era did mention my procurements during that time. There was a footnote in it that you turned me down on my offer."

"I did. I didn't need money then, and I don't need it now. If that's why you've come to see me again."

"I understand that you are a man of God, and such trivial things don't matter to you."

"It wasn't so much the bribe as it was your deception toward the bishop. You had no intent of donating money and land to the church as you promised him. You knew it as you spoke the words to him, and so did I."

Javier stared at him as if he didn't know what to say.

"I speak plainly Monsieur Garcia. There's no time for anything else."

A woman wearing black with a veil over her head walked into the chapel area and began lighting a candle.

"I see," Javier said stroking his trim beard. "Would it be possible to talk outside in the fresh air and sunshine? It is a glorious day."

Peter placed a cool gaze on him for a moment. "All right. I can tell that you will persist until I acquiesce, so let's get on with it."

Exiting through one of the west portal doors Peter walked toward Le Parvis, turned right on the rue du Cheval Blanc, and walked past the cathedral to a flight of steps leading to a labyrinth made of grass overlooking the Eure River. Javier followed at his side trying to make idle conversation.

"Another labyrinth outdoors?"

"It's smaller than mine but nice to walk in when the weather's good."

"Do you walk in yours every day?"

Peter ignored the question. When he reached the bottom of the stairs, he began his trek through the winding green path. Javier matched his steps a few feet behind.

"So, what do you want from me Monsieur Garcia?"

"It is me who would like to give you something."

Peter rolled his eyes but said nothing.

"In all of my lives, until now, I never had the honor of meeting and marrying my Grace. She is a lovely woman. And my children adore her."

"Did your queen die early again in this life?"

"Oh, it was so unfortunate. A plane crash. Into the ocean."

"Uh huh."

"But I found my Grace a few years later. And as I said, my children care deeply for her."

"How are your children? I hear that your older daughter is quite talented with her music compositions."

"She wastes her time with such worthless pursuits. This life she is rebellious and stubborn embracing societal extremes that don't bring honor to our house."

"Uh huh. I see," Peter said. "And your son, have you whipped him into shape?"

"Alejandro needs some guidance still, but he is a good son."

"Let's return to what you want from me."

"No. As I said, I want to give you something. A great gift. You see, my wife is the granddaughter of Louise Barbe. An alchemist at the dawn of the twentieth century. And her grandfather, while not officially documented, was no doubt Jean-Julien Champagne. Perhaps you have heard of his nom de plume of Fulcanelli."

Peter did not respond.

"Grace inherited the private library of her grandmother. And while I had been aware of alchemy in my previous lives, only the casual mention appeared in my diaries. My interactions up until this life dealt mainly with loaning money to academics like Isaac Newton who squandered much of his wealth on his futile pursuit of the great work."

At the center of the labyrinth Peter stopped. He inhaled deeply while looking out on the river below.

"And what has any of this to do with me, Monsieur Garcia?"

Javier stopped walking and turned to face Peter.

"I am from the Basque region. On the French side, but very close to the Spanish border. I am very proud of my heritage. We are a unique people sheltered for thousands of years from any outside influences. Our language is extraordinary. Very few can read it. But my son, Alejandro, wanting to impress me took up its study."

He looked down at his black Ferragamos again and chuckled. "He knew I had taken an interest in alchemy and had begun reading books from Grace's library. They were in French of course. The language both Louise and Jean-Julien wrote in."

Stroking his mustache, he continued. "But Alejandro, he discovered a letter written in my Basque language among the books and he translated it."

Javier caught Peter's gaze as it cut from the river toward him. It lasted only a moment before it returned to the river, but it was there. Peter stepped out of the center and began walking the path out of the labyrinth. Javier seemed to watch him carefully, but chose his next words even more carefully.

"The letter was from a monk who lived in Bilbao to his brother who lived in Paris. The year was 1418. How it came into the possession of Louise Barbe, I do not know."

The king of the house of Pentacles held up his hand to signal Peter, the Hanged Man of the tarot to stop walking. Peter stopped.

"The letter said that Nicolas Flamel, a resident of Paris, and the only known person to succeed in transmuting base metal into gold had given the secret to a priest in Chartres before he died."

Javier looked squarely into Peter's eyes, his gaze steady, unblinking. "That priest was you."

Peter stared at him giving no visual clues. "And?"

Javier squinted his eyes. "And so, Saint Peter, I am sure not only do you know what I just said is true, but you still possess this secret. You know what thousands have spent their entire lives trying to accomplish. You know how to turn metal into gold."

Peter stepped over the curved green patch of grass next to

his right foot to move away from Javier and continue his walk out of the labyrinth.

"As I said at the beginning of our conversation, I don't have any use for money. I don't want it or gold."

Javier followed Peter ignoring the path, stepping on the grass dividers and cutting across the labyrinth.

"And I believe that is precisely why Flamel gave the secret formula to you. Because he knew you wouldn't use it, but hide it from the world."

In four quick steps Javier bounded across the labyrinth to block Peter's exit.

"That is a cruel thing to do Saint Peter." A smile sliced across his face. "Do you know how many poor people I could help with knowledge such as that?"

"You would help yourself and no other. I know that." Peter walked around Javier, stepped out of the labyrinth, and headed for the stairs.

"I guessed this would be your reaction," Javier called after him. "So, I asked some associates to search your room at the Hôtellerie Saint-Yves."

No response came from Peter.

"I don't think they will find anything there, so I also asked them to search in the cathedral, including the crypt. There is a lot of handy work from your alchemist friends over the years down there."

Peter paused when he reached the top of the stairs by the *allée* of chestnut trees.

"You won't find what you're looking for. I promise you that." He turned and walked out of sight.

Javier sliced the smile across his face again. "Oh, yes I will."

Vesta could feel her breathing speed up. Forcing it to slow down, she said out loud, "Show me more."

The white canvas filtered into her mental space again

wiping clean the scene of Javier standing in the grassy labyrinth. Vesta waited in the blankness for the next InSight to come. A pain like the sensation of a stick being poked into her third eye caused her to wince.

"That hurts!" She physically rubbed the spot between her eyebrows. "What the hell!"

Willpower, coming instinctively from some place deep inside her, demanded that she keep her eyes shut. She knew something was trying to prevent her from seeing any more. No way would she lose the battle which she realized had commenced. Focusing her energy so it felt like a laser, she saw the sharp stick that jabbed her InSight come into view. She took hold of it with what looked like her hand and crushed it into dust, the particles scattering into the white mist.

"Show me more," she said in a slow, determined voice. Nothing happened. Vesta waited in the cloud for what seemed like minutes before taking a step to move around in the colorless, shapeless void.

"Ouch!"

Pain resonated somewhere within her. She looked down where her physical foot would have been and saw it hovering in the white space. Beside her foot lay a thick gray brick. As she watched, an identical brick began to form next to it.

"Absolutely not."

Her words echoed around the ether as she grabbed the two bricks with her hand and flung them into the air. They disappeared into the nothingness. From what she recognized as the vortex near her belly, searing energy burst forth blasting out a psychic barrier. Its protection surrounded her above, below, and all around. Pulsating energy surged through every cell. Victory was hers and she knew it.

"Now show me what I need to see."

A dark scene wobbled into her view.

"Lighten the picture," she commanded.

A golden glow expanded from a tiny dot in the middle of her view widening to encompass the entire scene. In the center was Peter, bent down next to the wall of the Well of Strong Saints in the Chartres crypt. Above him, she saw the mural on the ceiling of the hand reaching into the starry sky between the sun and crescent moon. Peter scratched at the base of the wall on the floor before stuffing something small into the pocket of his black pants.

"Show me a close up of what he's doing."

The omniscient eye obeyed moving closer. Too late. Peter stood up dusting off his slacks. He looked behind him before walking quickly out of the crypt into a starless night. The vision faded.

Vesta pressed her lips together and drummed her fingers on the rock before she spoke. "I want to see how Peter was kidnapped, from his point of view. Put me inside him at that moment."

The cosmic movie projector started rolling again. Peter was in Saint Piat's Chapel located behind the apse. Colorful abstract paintings hung on white stucco walls between the windows. Peter was walking along examining each piece of art, one by one, when a stocky man dressed as a priest entered the chapel through the small door from the cathedral stairway. He acknowledged Peter with a nod who responded with his own nod.

"Is this someone trying to imitate that painter Jackson Pollack?" the man asked as he walked up beside Peter.

"Oh, no. No one has been able to produce even a decent fake of his work." Peter turned to the priest who appeared to be in his twenties sporting a messy patch of blonde hair on his head. "You see, Pollack, whether he realized it or not mastered the art of fractals."

"Fractures?"

"Fractals. Patterns that recur at progressively smaller scales. It occurs constantly in nature, but he mastered it in his painting."

"Well, it just looks like a four-year-old got loose with some paint if you ask me."

Peter eyed the priest. "Are you new to the diocese? I don't think we've met before."

"Yeah, I guess you could say I'm new." He stepped close enough to Peter that the smell of cheap gin permeated his nostrils. A shiny object glinted in the morning sunlight as the priest pulled it from the pocket of his cassock.

"What is that? A knife?"

"That's what it is. A little insurance that you'll come with me. There's someone who wants to talk to you."

"Who?"

"You'll see."

"I'm not going anywhere. I'm not afraid of you."

"Okay. He said you might play it this way." The man who wasn't a priest pointed toward the door. "How about them? Are you willing to sacrifice somebody out there?"

"What are you saying?" Peter's eyes grew wide.

"I'm telling you that I'm going to cut at least one person, maybe more, if you don't come with me right now."

"You can't do that!"

"I can." the man said with a smile as he sliced the air with the knife. "And I will. Your choice."

"Why would you do that?"

"Because orders is orders."

"I'll call the police."

"Little good that would do. I'll be long gone before they hang up the phone. And those people's blood"—he pointed again toward the door—"will be on your hands."

Peter looked down at his hands. "I would never let that happen." He looked at the man pretending to be a priest. "Who wants to talk to me?"

"You'll see." The man motioned toward the door. "Time to go."

"Where are we going?"

"Too many questions."

"I don't want to leave the cathedral. I have work to do."

"It'll have to wait."

The man walked to the door and pushed it open with his foot. "Let's go, or I'll show you my own version of fractures."

Peter stared at him for a long moment, his gaze frozen like one of the statues on the choir screen in the apse.

"I," he stammered. "I can't go."

"Fine. Just remember, what's about to happen is all your fault."

The man pushed the door open as far as it would go. The ancient hinges let out painful creaks. Peter winced.

"Wait! Alright. I'll come with you."

"Good choice."

Peter ducked as he walked through the little doorway. He rubbed his hand against the jamb wood as he passed by as if to soothe a wounded soul. The man who was not a priest but dressed like one stood at the bottom of the staircase waiting for him.

"Okay. You be cool and nobody gets cut. Understand?"

Peter nodded.

"We'll go out that door over to the right."

The fake priest stayed close to Peter as they walked past the chapel holding the veil of the Virgin, past the Black Madonna and Child exiting by way of the north portal door. Early spring morning sunshine showered the pair as they turned right on the rue du Cheval Blanc and walked down the long stretch of old stone stairs at the end of the road. Near the bottom, a stone and brick bridge spanned the Eure River. Next to it stood Javier Garcia.

The man who was not a priest escorted Peter to Javier then retreated a few yards away and lit a cigarette.

"I'm not surprised it is you," Peter said.

"Did you really think our conversation was over?"

"What do you want?"

"You know precisely what I want," Javier said.

Peter lifted both arms out from his sides. "I don't have it anymore. I gave it away."

"Who did you give it to?"

Peter dropped his arms and shook his head. "I'm not going to tell you."

The pupils of Javier's eyes looked like two dark doorways opening to hell—fathomless, cold, and dead.

"You will," he said as he nodded toward the man dressed as a priest.

A black Mercedes Benz sedan pulled up at the bridge. The man opened the back door.

"Get in," Javier said.

"Into that car? No."

"You either get in, or Remy here will go back to your cathedral and follow through on his promise. And he'll drop your name as the sender of the tidings."

All the blood drained from Peter's face. His blue eyes stared from deep sockets. Long pale fingers hung limp from the bottom of their black turtleneck sleeves.

"I," he whispered. "I can't leave the cathedral." His eyes hurriedly glanced around him looking for some place to run.

"Get in," Javier repeated.

"Don't make me leave. Please."

"Then give me what I want."

"I don't have it any longer."

"Then who does?"

Peter bit his lower lip.

Javier motioned to Remy.

"Go do it." The man in the cassock ground out his cigarette on the street.

"No!" Peter said.

"I have no more patience to for this," Javier said. "You have two choices. Either tell me where the secret formula is, or get in the car. If you don't do either, then Remy will do exactly as I tell him."

Peter looked from Javier to the car. He didn't move.

"I will count to three," Javier said. "Then Remy will return to the church if you don't cooperate."

"Please don't. I can't leave my cathedral."

"One," Javier said in a bored tone. "Two, three," he continued in rapid succession. Remy began walking toward the stairs.

"Wait!" Peter exhaled. "I'll get into the car." His legs moved like they were made of jelly. He had almost no control over them, fearing at any moment they might collapse underneath him. As he reached the door, he grabbed the handle to steady himself, his hands sweating, slipping on the metal. Remy poked him on the shoulder with enough of a shove to send him careening into the backseat. His left arm trembled as he raised it to wipe the sweat from his forehead. The car door slammed shut. Javier slid into the seat beside him from the other open door. Remy took the front passenger's seat. A dark-skinned man that Peter could only see in profile was behind the steering wheel. He pressed on the gas pedal and drove over the bridge heading away from Chartres. A tear trickled down Peter's cheek.

Vesta squirmed on the rock; heat flared in her cheeks. The scene in her mind faded into the white mist.

"Show me where he is," she said. The blank mist continued to swirl. "Now!"

She sent the energy swimming around in her belly up through her heart, past her throat, and out of her third eye. Forms took shape out of the mist.

Peter sat at a simple desk looking out windows that appeared to be from the nineteenth century, newer than anything within Chartres cathedral. Red rimmed his blue eyes as though he had been crying for days. His scraggly light brown hair lay in frazzled clumps on his head while his black turtle-neck sweater and pants bore splotches of dried mud. He turned toward a curved staircase that terminated at a doorway of the small room. Javier descended the stairs toward him.

"Well, saint. Are you enjoying your accommodations?"

"I want to go home."

"Who has the secret formula?"

Peter turned back toward the windows. Javier looked down at a tray of uneaten food and smiled.

"Where am I?" Peter asked.

Javier, with his olive-toned skin looking fresh in his crisp white shirt, laughed.

"I chose some place very special. You like it here, no? The beautiful house and pond right by your door."

"I want to go home."

"You are in the writing studio of a famous author, Alexandre Dumas. Have you heard of him?"

"So, this is the Château de Monte-Cristo?"

"Ah, so you've heard of it."

"Actually, I knew the real life three musketeers his book was based on. They spent quality time at the cathedral once."

"This small chateau I purchased for special guests."

"You mean prisoners."

Javier laughed again. "Do you not think Monsieur Dumas would find the irony rather amusing?" He waved his hand around the room. "Château de Monte-Cristo with real prisoners, as you say?"

"He is probably cursing you from his grave."

Javier shrugged. "That is no concern of mine." He walked within an inch of Peter who didn't move or blink. "What does concern me is your reluctance to share your information."

A musky cologne wafted to Peter's nose. He could feel Javier's breath on his cheek.

"I'm losing my patience with you, saint."

"Nicolas gave me his notes to keep them safe from people like you."

"Did he tell you it would cost you your life?"

Peter stared unfazed. Javier waited for a reaction, but none came. He squinted. "You have the High Priestess looking for you now."

The gaze in Peter's eyes softened.

"Ah, so you were able to send a message even though I blocked her visions."

Javier stepped away from Peter and paced around the small room, his mouth puckering in erratic intervals.

"I suspect my disgrace of a daughter is somehow involved in this. That detestable noise she produces, you have somehow used to your benefit." He whirled around to face Peter. "Am I right?"

"Vesta is most capable on her own."

"She is a fool. And always has been. If Rasputin had left Raymond alone and not killed him, your priestess would never have known in this life what her true duty was. It was just luck, not experience, that allowed her to capture Valentina."

"They were murderers."

Javier cocked his head to one side and shrugged. "They did what they felt they needed to do. And Valentina knew exactly how to tell me to block the visions of the priestess."

"Valentina? You've been in contact with her?"

"Of course. She is a brilliant woman. Why wouldn't I ask her advice on something as important as finding the way to connect with God?"

Peter's eyes widened. "You think you'll connect with God this way?"

A deep laugh rumbled from Javier's mouth echoing off the plaster walls. "Saint Peter. Don't tell me you don't know."

"I know your quest for turning lead into gold or your stone heart into light isn't going to work."

Javier leapt toward Peter. "Yes, it will. There is no choice but for it to work when I have Flamel's instructions. All of this goodness and mercy that you care so much about does not factor into the equation. Don't you see? It's science. That's all that matters."

"God is love and mercy," Peter said as his eyes brimmed with tears.

"God is power," Javier sneered. "And that is all." He began pacing again.

"Once I build my own treasury from the gold I create, then I will turn my attention to the most significant matter."

His face went blank except for his eyes which opened wide. "I will become even better than you and the other major arcana." He looked down at his hands. "I will be immortal."

A gaping smile sliced across his face. "And I alone will give immortality to whom I choose."

Peter's face blanched an ashen color. "You can't do that."

The skin-crawling laugh returned. "I can. And I will." He approached Peter slowly. "Now it is time for you to tell me the secret or die."

"But if I die, the secret will die with me."

Javier shook his head. "I don't believe you." His eyes glanced around the room. "It exists somewhere. And you know where."

Again, his cologne and breath were pushing against Peter's face.

"If you don't tell me I will kill you, and then I will begin killing those who are in your precious cathedral just like Remy threatened to do. Except I will do it. Then I will find the formula even if I have to pull that church apart stone by stone." Javier glanced out the window. "Or maybe I will just blow it up and sort through the rubble."

Peter stood frozen. He didn't know what to say. The thought of returning in the next life without his cathedral was more than he could bear to imagine. Where would he live? Where would he find the spiritual salve that kept him going life to life? The blood in his veins felt like sludge and his eyes glazed over.

Javier turned from the window. "This is the last sunset you will see if you don't give me the formula. I will plant you next to your friend Flamel tomorrow if I don't have it."

The vision began to fracture and fade as Javier walked out of the room.

Vesta's breathing became fast and heavy. "Where is Nicolas Flamel buried?"

She asked the question out loud as though the trees or stream would answer. Pulling the earpieces out and scrambling off the rock, she ran through the slim opening between the boulders and back the way she came. When she burst into the circle clearing where Grace, Liam, Angeles, Luc, and Abby waited she was out of breath and close to tears.

"Where is Nicolas Flamel buried?" She blurted out the words as she approached them.

Each member of the little group looked around at the other for a few moments as though they were trying to make sense of her question.

"His headstone is at Musée de Cluny, but he isn't buried there," Abby said finally.

Grace moved closer to her. "Try to calm yourself. This state will serve no purpose for you." She stretched out her hand placing it on Vesta's. "His bones are lost to history."

"No! Somebody must know." Vesta wiped sweat from her forehead. "Javier knows because he's going to take Peter there tomorrow and kill him." She looked around the circle of faces. "Or today. What time is it?"

Luc checked her watch. "It's one-thirty."

"I have to get back to Paris to search for the tower."

"Wait," Grace said. She was staring at the ground. "I am trying to remember something from my grandmother's journals. It was about the funeral of Nicolas Flamel." She looked up at Vesta. "It mentions where he was buried." She shook her head. "But I can't remember where."

"Can we search her journals?"

"Of course."

"My InSight showed me Javier telling Peter that he wouldn't see another sunset. He intends to kill him today if he doesn't tell him Flamel's secret formula. And then he said he would begin killing people at Chartres cathedral." Vesta looked at Grace. "He's crazy and evil!"

Grace and Luc exchanged glances. "He clearly is," Grace said.

"Javier is holding him right now at Château de Monte-Cristo. Where is that?"

"Near le Port-Marly just outside of Paris," Grace said. "It's a neo-Gothic castle with beautiful grounds. Javier's consortium purchased it last year I think."

"Why don't you call the police and tell them to go there?" Luc asked.

"I have to make sure it's handled correctly. While they would probably check it out, Javier could hide Peter. Or kill him and then hide his body."

"Yes, that's true," Grace said. "Also, he is friends with many in the police department. Some do his bidding, I think."

Vesta frowned. "I have one chance to get it right. If I don't, Peter will die."

"I think Vesta is right," Liam said. "She has to do it."

"The train will take too long to get back to Paris." Vesta's voice cracked with pain as she spoke the last words.

"Oh, we'll make it," Liam said. "I'm not an international rock star beloved by millions for nothing." Vesta rolled her eyes in appreciation of his humor despite her own despair.

"I'm kidding!" he said to the others. "Well, not about being a rock star. Or being loved by millions. But my tone, I'm kidding about that."

"Liam!" Vesta shouted. "What are you trying to say?"

"I can get us a private plane pronto!" He pulled his cell phone out of his pocket. His hand waved it around in the air. "When I get a bloody signal, that is."

"Okay, so that will be the plan," Luc said. "Let's return to our hotels and Liam will let us know when we take off."

"You're all coming with me?" Vesta asked.

"Of course. We will each do our part to find Peter," Luc said.

Vesta smiled through the tears that had begun to run down her face. "Thank you. Let's hope Grace can find that journal."

Chapter Eleven

The waning moon hung high in the sky like a misshapen silver dollar. Participants from the night chant of the forest—still enjoying the afterglow from their alchemical adventure—danced and laughed in the clearing under its brilliant light.

"That lot will be here until the sun comes up," Liam said as he nodded toward them. "And under normal circumstances, I would be right there with them."

"You can stay," Vesta said.

"Oh no, no," Liam said as he began walking from the circle. "We must rescue old Peter. It creates a crack in the world when he dies any place other than his"—he gestured toward Vesta—"and your cathedral."

"What?"

Liam raised his eyebrows. "Turn of a phrase my pet. Let's get to a spot where I can find a bloody cell phone signal."

They led the way as Grace, Angeles, Luc, and Abby followed. The moonlight again seemed to shine a path for them threading through the towering red spruce. Voices in the circle suddenly fell silent.

"Why did they stop?" Vesta asked.

"They didn't," Grace spoke from behind her. "The circle is enchanted. Once you depart it, you can no longer hear the voices inside."

"It's a protection spell," Abby said. "I read about it in an old grimoire I found at the Warburg Institute a few years ago."

"A what? Where?"

Abby caught up with Vesta. "A grimoire is a book of magic and spells. Most are just fanciful fiction, but a few are the real deal."

"You mean like witches and magical spells? You're telling me things like that really exist?"

Abby smiled. "Is it any more surprising than you and Liam who are the living embodiment of tarot cards?"

Vesta shrugged as she followed the moonlit path. "I guess not. And not any more than this moonlight that's obviously showing us the way out of here."

"Exactly."

"How do you know so much about it? You don't study that at the Sorbonne, do you?"

"No." Abby shook her head. "One of my ancestors was accused of being a witch and was burned alive. So, I was curious to learn more about it."

"And you found it at some institute?"

"Yeah, the Warburg. Cool place. You should go sometime. The original tarot paintings by Lady Frieda Harris are there."

"I don't know who that is."

"She created what's known as the Thoth deck according to explicit instructions from Aleister Crowley. It's really beautiful, based on what is called projective synthetic geometry."

"Am I better dressed than in the Waite-Smith deck?"

The image Pamela Coleman-Smith painted of her was crude, to say the least, in Vesta's opinion. In the past six months, since she had become familiar with the Waite-Smith deck, she came to understand that the light blue dress she wore with the white cross emblazoned on the front Smith reproduced from original artwork created in the fifteen-hundreds of her. She really did dress like that during those days. Vesta grimaced at the thought.

"Oh, you look like a powerful Egyptian priestess," Abby replied.

"Good. I'll have to check it out some time."

"That stodgy image from Pamela gives no clue to the woman you are today," Liam called out as he led the pack.

"But yours still does," Vesta said in a light-hearted tone.

"I can rock a pair of tights when I choose."

"What about that little dog that's on your card with you? I've been meaning to ask. You've never owned a dog."

"Oh, you mean Plato. He's pure metaphor these days. Now it's my adoring fans who follow me obediently."

A groan went up from the entire group as Liam laughed. "Knew that reaction was coming."

The spot between Vesta's eyebrows began to tingle. No InSight came, but she knew it meant she needed to pay attention. She let Abby pass her falling to the back of the group. A detailed survey of the landscape around them showed there were only the spruce spires now quiet from their song. Nothing else. Silence pervaded the forest except for the crunching of six pairs of footsteps. Maybe, she was picking up Peter's energy again. Did he know she was coming to rescue him? Grace had to find the journal that mentioned the burial place of Nicolas Flamel.

The enchanted moonlight stopped when they reached the main trail. She looked up into the sky. High above the stars looked like Swarovski crystals dumped onto black velvet with the moon peeking out from behind the skyscraper grove of red spruce. They followed the trail to the road by the visitor's center. She turned toward the cluster of hotels a short walk ahead.

"I'll phone you for our departure time," Liam said.

She looked behind her. "Aren't you all going to your hotel?"

"We're staying at a villa by the river. Just around the corner."

Vesta raised her eyebrows. "Well that's nice."

"It's the perks you get when you're a legend and you come here every year."

"Whatever." Vesta turned back toward her hotel and continued her walk alone. The street was deserted except for a cat that slinked between two storefront doors. The darkened windows of the chalet style buildings looked like eyes that had closed for a peaceful night's sleep. She used her door key which doubled as the way to unlock the main door to the hotel lobby when she arrived. The clerk behind the reception desk raised his drooping eyelids to look at her as she passed.

Musty odors of old paint hit her nose as she walked into her room. Years of the same carpet and drapes shut out from fresh air would do that. Her third eye itched and tingled. She rubbed it as she looked at the combination radio alarm clock beside her bed. Three o'clock. The best thing would be for her to go to sleep immediately, but the spot between her brows was trying to tell her something. Probably that all the events of the evening needed to be analyzed so she could prepare for Peter's rescue.

She had noticed a sign for an indoor swimming pool earlier when she walked from her room to the restaurant. If her room key unlocked the main lobby door, then it would more than likely open the door to the pool. A lap or two would allow her to think and lay out a more detailed plan. From inside her suitcase she pulled out her black Norma Kamali one-piece swimsuit. She pulled off her clothes, pulled on the suit, slid into a pair of flip-flops she always traveled with, and grabbed a towel from the bathroom. In two minutes flat, she was out of the room.

The fluorescent lighting in the hallway was hideous as it spastically flickered making her eyeballs feel like they were wiggling as she made her way downstairs. When she opened the door to the enclosed pool area, a heavy dose of chlorine assailed her nostrils.

"Stop whining. Focus, Vesta. Focus," she said to herself as she kicked off the flip-flops and dropped the towel on a plastic poolside chair. "You're not here to bitch, but to plan."

She dove into the deep end and felt the soft warm water envelop her. "Ah," her brain murmured. The sensation was just what she needed.

Bobbing up to the surface, she began swimming toward the shallow end. The soreness and swelling on her injured ankle had disappeared, chlorine soaking the bandage, cleaning the wound. One controlled stroke after another let her thoughts leave her physical awareness and recap the evening.

Paneveggio Forest had turned out to be an enlightening experience even if Peter wasn't there. She now knew that Javier had found a way, with Valentina's help, to block her InSight. Yet Luc had created the path for her to regain it through her music. Why had he suggested that she come here? He wanted her out of Paris, that she knew. But he couldn't have had any idea of the revelations she would acquire sitting beside the stream, the destruction of the block he created, or he would have suggested someplace else. Luc wasn't supposed to be here. Javier thought she and Abby would be in Venice enjoying a holiday. It was Grace who called on her once she overheard Javier's comment to Alejandro.

Vesta felt the wall of the pool as her fingertips stroked it. After a quick rotation of her body, she headed back toward the deep end. Grace wasn't conspiring with Javier. That was certain. She had not only asked Luc to come to the forest with her InSight-stimulating music, but had traveled with only a moment's notice to warn her in person. Soft, warm feelings spread through her, and she was startled to realize that love existed in her heart for Grace. She smiled to herself. Elegant Grace, who dressed in white like her mother, had become a true friend. The only one she had ever had besides Liam.

Each lap in the pool brought more tingling to her third eye. At first it was an annoyance because she couldn't figure out why it was persisting. But the annoyance grew stronger and evolved into her sole focus. It was at that point she felt the prickly sensation on the back of her neck. When she reached the edge of the shallow end of the pool again, she stood up wiping the water from her eyes, determined to figure out what the message was.

"What are you trying to tell me?" She spoke out loud in an irritated voice to the buzzing spot between her eyebrows.

"We're going to see if you're a mermaid."

The shock of a gruff voice responding to her question when she thought she was alone was only eclipsed by the hard shove she felt on top of her head as it was plunged under water.

Vesta struggled to come up for air but the hand held a tight grip on her hair roots pushing her head against the concrete bottom of the pool. A small tsunami wave washed past her. She opened her eyes to see heavy work boots anchored on the bottom of the pool with jeans stuffed inside them squatting a few inches away from her. Punching with her fist at the groin of the pants did no good as water buffered the impact. Her hands reached for the pants waist to pull the man off balance but the hand that wasn't trying to drown her grabbed her right wrist and twisted it hard. Pain shot through her. And the realization that she was out of options.

Was this it? Once or twice she had imagined how she would die, old and alone in her bed, childless and unmarried had come to mind before, but never at the shallow end of a rundown indoor pool in the middle of nowhere in Italy. Enid had taught her how to swim during the warm summer months in Crested Butte. Vesta's thoughts flashed to those days. The cold mountain water glinting on the surface from the bright sunshine as she dove deep down for small beautiful rocks on the bottom of the pond. Enid told her to always calm her mind while holding her breath because that would allow a longer time before the next breath was necessary.

"Panic is never your friend," was a familiar phrase from Enid.

Calm down, she told herself. Go limp, she demanded. Don't fight. Everything within her wanted to fight, but her only chance was not to. She forced every muscle in her body to relax, double checking to make sure they stayed that way. Her focus was on overcoming her thoughts. Enid said that most people didn't realize that the average person could hold their breath for four minutes without any problems. Think of the pearl divers, she had said. Vesta recalled photographs of pearl divers she had seen in one of her school books. They could dive to great depths staying underwater for seven or eight minutes. It was because they learned to take charge of their minds, Enid explained. That was what she must do. She was a pearl diver going to the bottom of her psyche to retrieve the most valuable part of herself. Turn loose of the fear, she demanded. It was only a learned response, a surface reaction. Go deeper. Remember who you are.

At last, her urge to breathe abated while the big hand kept her head steadfast on the floor of the pool. Seconds crept by like lifetimes as she lay floating as lifelessly as possible in the now calm pool. Her chin scraped against the cement as the meaty hand slightly shifted positions on top of her head. Don't struggle. There was no way she could overpower this hulking assassin. She had to stick with her plan and if it didn't work, she would die. That meant she wouldn't save Peter from being murdered. Anxiety began to creep in.

She commanded her mind to go blank. The white cloud she had witnessed earlier in the night while sitting on the boulder listening to Luc's music came swirling back into view. From the mist, the image of the heavy work boots and jeans faded into focus with a torso and head attached. She looked at the ruddy red face with the dark stubble of hair on his head and chin. It looked like the nose had been smashed more than once and not repaired. A pair of beady dark eyes stared at her.

"Your name is Jacques," she said to him in her mind. "I know that." Her gaze shifted to the lower right side of his body. Through the jeans and plump white skin, she could see a small area inside the abdomen glowing red.

"Ah!" Adrenaline flooded through her. "And I know that your appendix is ready to rupture." All she had to do was stay calm and wait in the tranquil void.

At last, the pressure on her head lessened. She could feel the large fingers slightly release their grip on her hair. Stay limp, she told herself as awareness of the swimming pool returned. How many minutes had she been underwater? There was no way to tell but the anticipation of breathing air again, taking a huge breath into her lungs, made her almost tighten a muscle or two, but she caught herself. Stop! Leave the body alone. Forcing herself to comply with the command, she turned her attention away.

Her awareness shifted. She saw the pool from above. White plastic chairs stacked one on top of the other stood in a corner, others were scattered around the side of the pool. One had her towel draped over its arm and a pair of flip-flops sitting underneath. A Styrofoam ring large enough for a person to float in, or be rescued by, lay against the beige tile wall. The heavy odor of chlorine hung in the air.

Inside the pool, a heavyset man in jeans and work boots held a woman with short bleached blonde hair wearing a black Norma Kamali one-piece swimsuit under water at the shallow end. Some part of Vesta regarded the scene with no emotion even though she knew she was witnessing the last moments of her life. The man looked up toward the door, turned loose of the woman and stood up.

Sharp concentration raced back into her body. She would get only one shot. Her eyes opened and she watched. Wait, she told herself. One of the work boots moved to step out of the pool. The man with the red, ruddy face for the next second would be standing only on his left foot.

"Now!" she screamed inside.

Using all the energy within her, which was shockingly diminished she realized, she grabbed the waistband of the jeans with both hands. She pulled down as hard as she could. Like a slow-motion scene from some movie she had long forgotten, the legs and torso toppled into the water causing a shockwave across the pool. Vesta shot above the surface. Her mouth opened gulping in air. Chlorine stung her lungs, and she began to cough. As she opened her eyes the chlorinated water clouded her sight. She wiped away the water with both hands then lunged for the man.

His face changed from surprise to anger within a split second. The tiny black dots that were eyes widened.

"You bitch!" He reached for her as he scrambled to stand up as furious little waves lapped against him.

Vesta spotted her target and drove her right foot with all the force she had into the right side of his abdomen. Even though several inches of water covered his body which would soften the blow, when the sharp wedge of her bony heel struck the padded flesh, she could feel the satisfying impact. He howled as his hands reached out for her. Air flowed easily in and out of her lungs. Never had anything felt so good. Her vision was clear. She raised her leg again and aimed. With one swift motion she brought the heel of her foot down on the soft spot of the man's belly once more.

A sickening sound, some mixture of a screech and a cry, bellowed out of him. His arms and legs went limp, his eyes glazed over no longer looking at her. Vesta grabbed the collar of his blue shirt and dragged him to the steps in the corner. She propped his head above the water on the edge of the pool. His body bobbed with the waves lapping against the bank.

"Who sent you Jacques?" The man's eyes looked toward her but gave no response. "It was Javier, wasn't it?" Vesta squinted her eyes and smiled at him. "Well I'll be seeing Javier soon enough. And I'll give him your regards."

"It hurts," Jacques mumbled.

"Oh, I know." Vesta stepped out of the pool, picked up her towel and slid into her flip-flops. She turned around and looked at the man whose body floated aimlessly in the water.

"Someone will come for you. You're not worth killing this time." Vesta could hear a low moan as she opened the door and walked out into the hallway.

Inside her room, the radio alarm clock displayed the time in red—four-sixteen—and the message light on her mobile phone was blinking. She sat down on the bed and played the message as she softly touched the raw patch on her chin. Liam's voice came through the tiny speaker saying to meet at the visitor's center at nine o'clock. From there they would drive to Venice, return rental cars and board a private plane at Marco Polo airport by twelve-forty-five.

Five hours to wait. Vesta drummed her fingers on the bed as she looked around the room. A shower was necessary. Maybe she would lay down for an hour after that. Coffee should be available somewhere downstairs by six. That would give her enough time to consider all possible scenarios that she could face that day and how she would handle each one. She nodded and smiled.

Another hideous fluorescent light in the bathroom exposed the red patch of skin on her chin when she gazed in the mirror. It was swelling too, but nothing that makeup wouldn't hide. Vesta stepped into the small prefabricated shower, the water washing away the chlorine and any remaining doubt about her capabilities. Tonight, she had integrated her High Priestess InSight with her survival instincts as a girl who grew up on the side of a mountain. A smile drifted across her face as she shampooed her hair. They worked well together. She paused. They combined to save her life. One wouldn't have been sufficient. Both were necessary. Deep inside she knew a milestone had been reached, a corner turned in this life.

Stale dampness had soaked the walls of the bathroom for so many years that it left a permanent imprint. Vesta quickly dried off to get away from the musty odor and cloying tiny room as fast as possible. She walked to her suitcase and stared at it. A long day loomed in front of her, proper attire was necessary. Despite the gravity of the moment she couldn't help but smile to herself. Most people in her situation wouldn't give more than a second's thought to what they would wear. Grab a shirt and pair of pants and be done with it. That was impossible for her. Since the days of gazing at Vogue crouched by the magazine rack in the grocery store in town, she had cared deeply about what she wore. What she put on would be practical, of course, but also an outfit that instantly communicated who she was to all who would see her. To do anything less was unthinkable. Clothing identified who she was just like it showed who everyone else was whether they realized it or not. It was a symbol of their inner self as much as the outer, their persona, their self-respect. Vesta had always known that. Over the years she realized that she could gauge who a person really was by their appearance. The old saying that a book couldn't be judged by its cover was flawed. She knew that intuitively.

From her suitcase she pulled out a pale gray Calvin Klein cashmere sweater set and a pair of his dark gray trousers. That would take her from early morning to late at night, if need be. She got dressed and picked up the necklace from Liam laying on the beside table. As she placed it around her neck, she caught her image in the mirror hanging over the beaten-up chest of drawers. The crescent moon dangling from the string of misshapen stones glinted in the light. Picking up her bath towel she began polishing the stones for a few moments. Even though it was not a lovely piece of jewelry, deep grooves scratched into odd-sized mismatched stones, the necklace had become a treasured part of her wardrobe that she was fine wearing every day for a while. It felt more than good to have it on.

She combed back her short bleached blonde hair to let it dry naturally. One of the best hair styles she had ever selected, quick and outrageously easy. Dabs of concealer and powder to cover the bright pink patch of skin on her chin, mascara and lipstick and she was ready. Slinging the thin long strap of a small Chanel purse across her body she gazed in the mirror one final time before leaving the dumpy room. She felt satisfied with how she had melded her worlds. Amara once told her that in previous lives she had never cared about what she wore. Indeed, seeing a previous incarnation of herself through her InSight during a mind-bending time lapse in the labyrinth one day, she saw herself in a pale blue robe with an enormous white cross embroidered on the chest. Vesta smoothed her sweater, straightened her cardigan and smiled at her image. That may have been fine for her in medieval France but not for today.

She closed her suitcase, set it on the floor and rolled it out the door, turning out the horrible wiggly blue fluorescent light in the damp bathroom as she left.

Chapter Twelve

A t seven-thirty someone from the hotel finally brought a pot of coffee into the dining room. She had waited for an hour and a half in her dead-tired physical state. Mentally she wasn't much better. Vesta took a cup from her table, walked to the coffee station and filled it to the brim. At least Italian coffee was more like espresso. She needed it. After her shower, getting dressed, including camouflage for the raspberry on her chin, and packing her bag she came down to the lobby. To her reasoning it was a combination of restlessness and security. Sleep wasn't an option when her thoughts were moving so fast and were so jumbled. Add to that the slight possibility that another attacker might arrive at her room. The best idea was to wait in the lobby.

It turned out to be a well-timed decision because evidently a housekeeper beginning her duties for the day found Jacques in the pool. Vesta saw the thin middle-aged woman in the black work dress skitter down the hall from the pool area. Her Italian was rapid as she rattled off a stream of indecipherable words to the sleepy clerk at the reception desk. But her excited gestures pointing toward the pool explained the situation to Vesta. The clerk picked up the phone and spoke to someone. Fifteen minutes later two men arrived wearing a combination of what appeared to be nightshirts and dark slacks, their hair disheveled. They sped an old hospital gurney from probably World War II past her toward the pool.

Several minutes passed before they wheeled Jacques in soaking wet clothes out the main door. His eyes closed, his pale face breathing heavily. Vesta watched the trio and wondered what story he would concoct to explain why he was in the pool, fully dressed, so early in the morning.

Residual chlorine from the swimming pool water still clung in places inside her throat and made the first sip of coffee sting as it slid down. But the second was true pleasure.

"Yes," she cooed as the jolt took hold.

The previous night had been a turning point for her. Not only did she figure out how to demolish the psychic blocks Javier erected preventing her InSight, but she came very close to drowning. Had she not used survival skills taught to her as a child she would not be sitting in the restaurant planning out her day? Since the time of Rasputin's stooge shooting Uncle Raymond, killing him on the parapet of the Casteel del Papa Luna in Spain, when with his dying words he told her about the spell she cast on herself, she had felt a deep disconnect between who she thought she was and who she had been for dozens of lifetimes. For the first time since, she felt the two lives unite. She was the High Priestess of the trionfi, but she was also Vesta—the scrawny kid who lived in a cabin on the side of Crested Butte mountain who knew how to survive in the modern world.

One more gulp of coffee drained the cup dry. She walked to the silver thermos pitcher and poured another. All of her skills would be required within the next twelve hours to rescue Peter. Caffeine coursed through her body as she poured another cup down her throat. She knew she could settle the buzz to call on her InSight. No warning signs were coming from her third eye which she would trust from now on as her barometer of things that needed her immediate attention. She sat down at the table and closed her eyes. With a clear intention she directed the rush she felt in her physical body to obey her command to transform from frenetic energy into focused mental sharpness. Inhaling long and deep, she instructed the scattered sparks to coalesce into a blue-white ball of vibrant power she could see in her mind.

"Ah," she murmured when she felt it take root in her forehead. Letting out the breath slow and steady, she was ready to begin.

"Peter, are you okay for the moment?" Her fine-tuned sensitivity stretched out into the realm where distance and matter have no meaning. The little bicycle wheel between her eyebrows began a slow, warm spin.

"Vesta!" The response was immediate and a bit startling to her.

"Are you okay?" Energetic fingers that she imagined as impossibly long and delicate like the ones of deep-sea jellyfish stretched out further toward him.

"I'm alive but my soul is evaporating without my cathedral."

"I know. I'm coming to get you."

"Thank you. Please hurry."

"Where is Javier taking you? I know it's a tower, probably in Paris."

"I don't know."

"Alright. I have a plan to find you."

"I feel so lost."

Vesta could see only a dark silhouette of Peter's tall, thin frame lying on a floor.

"I will find you. And before sunset."

"You are my champion," he said as dark swirls overtook her view.

The spinning of her third eye stopped and Vesta opened her eyes. Two people, speaking German, had entered the restaurant and were sitting at a table by the wall. She looked at her watch. It was almost eight. Deciding one more cup of coffee wouldn't hurt, Vesta found a paper cup near the pitcher and filled it full. She walked back to her table as a waiter carried in a tray of sliced meat and cheese. She slung the Chanel purse across her body, pulled up the handle of her Sybarite luggage and walked to the main door.

"Ciao," a new clerk looking rested and fresh called out from the reception desk.

"Ciao," Vesta replied as she pushed open the door walking away from a night she would never forget and a bed she never slept in.

Soft daylight filtered through the mountains tip-toeing toward the town to gently wake sleeping guests in their rooms as she walked to the parking lot. An hour would pass before the bright ball of yellow sun would be visible over the peaks and the chill of night would loosen its grip. A shiver ran through her body. She wasn't sure if it was because her Sybarite sweater set she chose to wear was too lightweight or because subconsciously she understood how close she came to dying in that random hotel.

Vesta shook her head to jar the thought from her mind as she reached the car. After fishing out the key, she popped open the trunk to deposit the luggage then settled into the driver's seat. Almost an hour remained before she would meet Liam and the group, but she had to at least get away from this place.

The visitor's center sat on the right less than a mile away. A bicycle leaned against a wall of the building in an otherwise empty parking lot as she pulled in and got out of the car. Wind rustled through the needles of the red spruce that surrounded her. Close by the sound of water splashed against boulders in the river. Vesta walked to the bridge that lead to the main path. She knew that the weak plank on the bridge the day before wasn't an accident. Nor was the car that almost hit her as she crossed the street. Javier had sent Jacques to kill her. He dangled the hope of finding Peter here but his real intent was to isolate her in a remote place so she could be murdered.

He underestimated her. And she would show him just how much. Unconsciously she rubbed on the misshapen stones of the necklace Liam had given her. Had it only been a week since they dined at Le Bernardin? Only a week since she found out about Peter's kidnapping, the loss of her InSight, meeting the trionfi family of Pentacles?

"Wow," she murmured to herself.

"I do elicit that response from a lot of women."

Vesta whirled around to see Liam striding up beside her, cigarette in hand, dressed in solid black, button-down shirt, jeans, and boots. His Fool medallion swayed from its leather cord on his semi-bare chest.

"You're early."

"I'm not the brekkie type. You know that. Instead of eggs, sausages, and the like, I'd rather have this." He waved his Marlboro in a circular motion. "And what about you? You must be ready to get the hell out of here."

"More than you know. I took a swim last night at the hotel pool and one of Javier's goons tried to drown me."

"Glad you're still with us."

"Me too."

"I told you that he was one to watch. He'll make good on dispatching Peter too if we can't save him."

"I know, but I will."

"You sound certain."

"I've gained a new level of mastery in the last twenty-four hours."

"Careful polishing that hubcap diamond star halo of yours. You might drop it."

"Stop using those old rock song lyrics on me."

"T-Rex and Marc Bolan are ageless. Lord rest his soul."

Vesta turned back to look at the river. "I have a plan."

"I hope you're right." Liam dropped his cigarette and ground it out with the toe of his boot. "Because you know gold isn't all that Javier can gain with that alchemy formula."

"Immortality too, right?"

"Yeah, dark souls come from that process."

Vesta looked at Liam. "You mean it's actually been done on humans before?"

"Oh, yes." Liam nodded. "And with very poor results." He pulled another Marlboro out of the pack in his shirt pocket along with a Bic lighter. "Difficult to kill those. Nasty tempers too when you try but fail."

Vesta's mouth fell open, she wanted to say something but couldn't quite decide what she wanted to say first, so she stared at Liam for a long moment. "Are there any alive now?"

"Very few," Liam said with the cigarette poised between his teeth as he lit it. He inhaled and let the smoke flow slowly out of his mouth. "They know the rules. Getting out of line will bring them the same fate as the others."

"So how do you kill someone who is immortal? Because they're different from us, right? We can be killed like regular humans, but they can't."

"More or less," Liam cocked his head.

"Wait, what? What's more or less?"

"We can be killed like RanChan most of the time. There are exceptions."

Vesta shook her head. "Okay, now you're confusing me."

"For your purposes right now, it's important for you know that those who have successfully transmuted themselves into the immortal state are very difficult to kill when they cross societal boundaries."

Liam flicked his cigarette. "It takes an expert."

"There's someone, like a bounty hunter, who tracks them down?"

Liam nodded. "Yep." He looked at her and grinned. "Your father."

Again, Vesta's jaw dropped open as she tried to form words. She blinked a couple of times putting her thoughts together. "Cyrus," she said finally. "Cyrus is a zombie killer."

Liam swooped a handful of brown, moppy hair out of his eyes and shrugged. "They aren't zombies, per se, but yeah, he's the one to call when the need arises." He cocked his head. "He handles other world crises as well, of course. That's why he wasn't around much when you were young."

An old familiar feeling of sadness mixed with anger washed from Vesta's heart to her belly. Memories of being fatherless and poor flooded into her thoughts. Since she had become aware of who she was among the trionfi, who her mother and father were —represented as Strength and the Chariot respectively—she tried to let go of her feelings of anger toward Cyrus. Even though he was busy carrying out his duties, she still possessed a deep sense of abandonment that she never fully turned loose of. She pushed the thoughts aside.

"Sounds like he has a big job," she said in dismissive tone despite not wanting to sound petty.

"He does." Liam wagged his finger at her. "And you have a big one too, today. Don't let the wanker get that formula or kill Peter in some random place." Liam took a long drag of his cigarette and let it out in a smooth current of white smoke. "He doesn't care if he dies, he just wants it to be at Chartres cathedral." He dropped the cigarette, ground it out with his boot and picked up both butts. "You see lovey, when you designed that place for him you bound his soul with it. Another alchemical process that I don't think you were quite aware of at that point. He had felt adrift for centuries. Once he had followed through on the wishes of his spiritual master, he didn't know what to do with himself. The religious group that grew from it was huge and powerful. Still is. But there was no place for him, really." He pitched the cigarette butts in a metal garbage can beside the bridge. "So, you built him one."

Grace, Angeles, Luc, and Abby emerged from around the corner of the visitor's center.

"Good morning," each called out.

Vesta nodded her head toward the group. She looked back at Liam. "I won't let him die today."

"Is everyone ready for our big adventure?" Liam asked.

"Waiting for you," Luc said with a smile.

The group piled into the two cars and drove out of San Martino di Castrozza, through the winding roads carved between the Dolomite mountains and the red spruce that festooned them. Vesta drove her rental car with Grace riding in the front seat beside her. Angeles sat behind them writing in a notebook along the way.

"Are you writing about our episode last night? It's supposed to be a secret though, right?" Vesta asked.

"None of that secret ceremony will be revealed by me," Angeles said. "I'm an anthropologist who researches diverse cultures, both modern and ancient." She leaned forward from the backseat. "I've come to realize that we have a dialogue between our internal and external worlds that is communicated by symbols. I'm making notes about how that translates into our lives today. You and the other members of the trionfi represent fundamental archetypes to our human psyches. You are living symbols."

"How long have you known about us?"

Angeles looked at Grace then back toward Vesta. "A long time. People don't need to know that you exist in a physical form in our present time. But they do need to understand what you represent."

"I guess our secrets are safe with you."

"They are very safe," Grace said. "Angeles makes people in this world aware of their own motivations and reckless tendencies. She is here to heal and help."

Grace patted Angeles on her hand that was lying on the center console.

"She is the best thing that came from my marriage to Javier. He introduced us."

"You were mixed up with Javier?" Vesta glanced for a second toward Angeles.

"Only because we are both from the Basque region and hold a special place in our hearts for it. He was actually the first person I suspected of being a living part of the tarot. His characteristics and motivations so clearly aligned with the King of Pentacles."

"We became good friends during the dinner parties at our home in New York. The ones Javier hosted for his Basque group. And I confessed that her suspicions were true."

"Did Javier tell you about all about the trionfi before or after you were married?"

"After, but like Angeles, I suspected something was unique about him and his daughters."

"And you married him anyway?" Vesta asked.

Grace shrugged. "There are stranger things in the world."

Vesta nodded, satisfied with the answer. A shiver ran up her spine as she thought of Javier and what he wanted to do with the alchemy formula. Where was it anyway? She hadn't asked Peter during their InSight conversations. Nicolas Flamel gave him the secret to keep it away from those who would use it. He trusted that Peter would guard it well. Wherever it was, Vesta knew it was safe.

They arrived in Venice a few minutes before eleven-thirty. Vesta dropped Grace and Angeles along with their luggage at the private section of the airport. She returned the rental car and took the shuttle to meet them. Everyone was in the lounge for passengers flying on chartered planes. A cluster of young women returning home to Tokyo had discovered Liam and were surrounding him with choruses of giggles and camera flashes. He was clearly soaking up their admiration and didn't notice Vesta's entry. Grace and Angeles sat next to each other talking in quiet voices. Luc and Abby were drinking champagne at the bar. Her mouth watered unconsciously. What an absolute loser she was. How could she possibly want a drink when her friend's life was at stake and she had assumed the responsibility to save him?

Shame, guilt, and also an unquenched desire which she loathed to admit, but was there, bubbled up inside her as she turned her gaze away from the bar and toward the wall of windows looking out on the tarmac. A young man with dark hair slicked back to reveal a pair of large brown eyes wearing a crisp white shirt and a navy jacket with matching pants, probably Armani, walked down the steps from a small jet and into the lounge. In perfect English tinged with an Italian accent he introduced himself to the room as the copilot of the flight departing for Paris.

Luc and Abby tipped their flutes to their lips to drain them. The Japanese women made sounds of disappointment while they clutched their cameras for one more piece of documented evidence with Liam. Angeles walked over to take photo of the entire group with their rock star.

One by one, each person boarded the jet. Vesta paused as she stepped through the doorway. The interior of the plane was bathed in black and gold leather. Medallions sporting golden Medusa heads were embossed on the headrests of every seat. In that moment, she realized she had guessed incorrectly about the designer of the copilot's suit.

"Good day." A male voice spoke behind her. Vesta sat down on a banquette and looked his way.

"I am Vincenzo Andrighetti. I am your captain today. It is the extreme pleasure of Senora Versace to welcome you aboard as her guests. Please let Carina know if there is anything you would like to make your flight to Paris more comfortable or enjoyable. My copilot Renaldo and I will be available also if you have any questions. I invite you to take your seats now as we are ready for departure."

Vincenzo turned around heading for the cockpit as a dark-haired beauty dressed in a crisp white blouse, navy skirt and jacket with a small gold medusa medallion pinned to her lapel walked in to greet them with a bottle of vintage Dom Pérignon.

"May I offer anyone a glass of champagne?"

Despite her best efforts, Vesta could feel her salivation glands kick into gear as she looked at the bottle. Nothing would be more perfect than to sip a glass of champagne on take-off from Venice in Donatella Versace's sumptuous plane. Fantasies were composed of scenes like this. But that was the old Vesta, she chastised herself.

"I would love one, absolutely!" Liam's cheerful voice called out from the back.

Walking to the galley at the rear of the jet Carina wheeled out a gold cocktail cart with six crystal flutes accompanied by the champagne in a silver ice bucket. Everyone took a glass except for Vesta who shook her head.

"No," she said. "Pellegrino for me, please."

Carina brought a crystal high ball glass filled with the sparkling water, set it on the table in front of Vesta. She then knocked twice on the cockpit door and took her seat for take-off. The jet moved slowly from the terminal, waited briefly for a Lufthansa 747 to lumber down the runway then revved its engines and sped into the sky.

While one glass of champagne during a two-hour flight wouldn't make her drunk or even tipsy, she knew the alcohol diluted, maybe even twisted, her abilities. Warning signs of addiction had popped up for years, but she kept them well under control and hidden from sight. She had relied on alcohol to smother emotional pain and loneliness since college. Having a drink, or two, or three substituted for relationships, friendships, or growing close to anyone.

Vesta drummed her fingers on the seat. She could have a drink after she rescued Peter, but not before.

Once at cruising altitude Grace walked from her seat at the back of the plane to sit on the banquette beside Vesta. She handed her almost full glass of champagne to Carina.

"I only wanted a sip to taste that particular vintage. It was pleasant. Hints of vanilla and *pamplemousse*, ah, how do you say it?"

"Grapefruit."

"Yes, grapefruit. Thank you."

Grace placed her hand on Vesta's in such an easy, natural way that Vesta wasn't repelled by it as she normally would be from someone like Amara. Instead, it felt reassuring and steady.

"Now, tell me how you would like to proceed when we arrive in Paris."

Vesta smiled at Grace. Dressed in a tailored white Yves

Saint Laurent jacket, blouse, and pencil skirt. In simple Laboutin black pumps with her wisps of short black hair and dark eyes framing her pale face, she looked like she was cut out from a black and white film from the nineteen forties and pasted in the seat next to her. A glamourous movie star brought to life.

"I would like to go immediately to your house to search for the book or diary that holds the location of Nicolas Flamel's burial site. Do you recall any details about what the exterior of it looked like?"

Grace glanced out the window, her eyes staring at the puffs of white clouds sailing past them. Several moments ticked by before she shook her head.

"I'm sorry. It was such a long time ago."

"Okay. Let's approach it from a different angle. When you told me that you had once read about the location, do you recall what memory came up? There must have been a moment that popped into your mind. Something that caused you to remember seeing it once."

Grace stroked her chin with her finger as her attention shifted to the glass of Pellegrino like it was a crystal ball. She stared at it for several moments before she spoke.

"It was not long after Javier and I were married, maybe five years ago." Her gaze wandered over to Vesta searching her face as if the answer lay somewhere between her eyes and nose.

"He was very interested in my grandparent's diaries and laboratory notes, reading for hours—days—with papers scattered everywhere in the library. It was to the point that his hip, the one injured in a motorcycle accident when he was younger and is now much weaker than the other, was unable to take the constant sitting."

Grace moved her gaze back to the Pellegrino. "After that he would pace around the room while he had me sit at his desk and summarize what I found in the papers he placed in front of me.

That was when I came across the reference. But I don't recall exactly what I was looking at."

"Okay. Good. That's a start." Vesta drummed her fingers her lap. "Do you think Angeles can help us look, to save time?"

"Unfortunately, not. She has to fly to New Orleans in a matter of hours after we arrive. There is a tribe of Indians there, the Mardi Gras, she is meeting with." Grace raised her eyebrows and said, "It sounds like a fun group, *n'est ce pas?*"

"It does. Okay. No problem." Vesta's thoughts raced on. "What about Luc and Abby? Would they help?"

"I think they would be happy to do that. I will ask them."

Vesta leaned back on the banquette exhaling. "Alright, then that will be our plan. We will find the location of his burial and I will be there before sunset."

"You will alert the police, yes?"

"I don't want to scare Javier away so that he takes Peter to another unknown location. And then there's the whole issue of trying to explain it to the police and them allowing me to be present if they do believe me and decide to go there." Vesta shook her head. "They will complicate everything, actually."

"Oh no, Vesta. You cannot go there alone. Javier is a dangerous man. He does not value human life." Grace looked down in her lap. "I learned that after we were married, otherwise I would have never consented, especially so quickly after meeting him."

"You married him soon after meeting him?"

Grace nodded. "He was extremely romantic. So handsome and kind. I could not believe such a person existed." A sad smile slid across her beautiful face. "I guess he really didn't exist after all."

Vesta reached out and touched Grace's hand. The unconscious action surprised her because she couldn't remember ever doing that before to anyone, except her mother.

"Don't worry. You don't have to stay with him. And there may be someone else come along in your life who really is what Javier appeared to be. You deserve that."

Grace smiled at Vesta. "You are so strong, yet sensitive. A true intuitive priestess of the highest order."

Vesta could feel warm, soft energy radiate from her heart up through her throat to her eyes. She wondered if she was going to cry, not because she was sad or angry, but because she felt such love for Grace.

Her friend squeezed her hand gently. "I will leave you to your thoughts but please let me know if there is anything I can do." Grace stood up and walked to join the others near the rear of the plane.

Vesta nodded. She needed to check in with Peter to tell him she was on her way to find him. Leaning her head back, she closed her eyes.

"Let me see Peter." The silent command echoed in her mind.

As she inhaled deeply and let it out, an image formed of him still lying on the floor of the small, sparse room at the Château de Monte-Cristo. Javier entered with the hulking man whom she knew was called Remy. He hoisted Peter up by his arm holding him in front of Javier.

"Where is the formula, saint?"

"It's gone. You'll never have it."

"There is no one coming to save you. Even if that feeble-minded priestess of yours does find a way around my block of her visions, I have someone there in the forest who will send her into her next life."

"I won't give you anything."

Javier gave a quick nod to Remy who delivered a hard slap to Peter's face. Bright red color flooded onto Peter's cheek, but he said nothing.

"Why go through all this pain? I will return you to your precious church. All I want is that formula. Jean-Julien knew it, didn't he? But someone tore the pages from his diary. Who did that?"

He glanced toward Remy again who punched Peter in the stomach, his thin skeletal frame reacted with a cracking sound. Vesta winced as she heard what she knew was a rib breaking. Drool slid out of the side of Peter's mouth as he drooped to the floor, suspended only by his arm held tight by the thug who had pretended to be a priest.

"Talk to me, Saint Peter. You don't want to die away from your church, do you? You will tonight if you don't tell me what I want to know. And I will have no ties to your death. You see, I know how to arrange things so they appear as accidents. Just like my first wife. Although, for you, it will be a tragic suicide."

"You're a monster."

A smile sliced across his face showing a glimpse of white teeth. "I know how to get what I want. All these lifetimes, and it was only in this one that I learned immortality is possible for me. To no longer rely on those diaries, all those years of relearning, wasted time. With Flamel's secret, the secret that Jean-Julien rediscovered, I will be even better than you. I won't die at all." Javier leaned close to Peter's face. "And I will be richer than any man in the world."

Laughter oozed out of Javier like sewage leaking from a rusty pipe, slow and rancid.

"And if you don't give me the formula, I will not only see you die, but I will send Remy to kill those who visit your church. One by one, accidents, suicides, crimes of passion, I can be very creative. Soon your precious Chartres cathedral will be associated with a curse."

Javier cocked his head letting the hollow smile smear across his face again. "Yes, I like that idea very much. I can be like your

God deciding the fate of all those parishioners and visitors." He raised his eyebrows. "And priests too, of course."

"May my God have mercy on your evil soul. I will never give you what you want."

The pupils of Javier's eyes narrowed as he stared at Peter for several moments before he spat on his face, white foamy liquid landing near Peter's eye. "That's what I think of you and your God."

He looked at Remy and jerked his head toward the wall. The man shoved Peter against it, crumpling him into a thin tangle of black arms and legs on the floor. Dark clouds filled the scene in Vesta's mind obscuring her view until it was entirely lost.

When she opened her eyes, she realized she had tears dried on her cheeks. Cold hate filled her senses. Inside the plane near the back she could hear Liam laughing that silly laugh of his. It brought her back to the present moment. She turned to look at the group. As usual Liam was holding court with all four women listening to him weave a tale of some misbegotten adventure. Vesta looked down in her lap. She would wait until they landed before she told Luc and Grace about Javier's murder of Xuxa, or Lily as she like to be called. The women needed to know. It wouldn't be right to keep the information to herself.

For the remainder of the flight Vesta gazed out the window, occasionally paying attention to the changing landscape below. The jagged Pyrenees mountains gave way to the expansive green of undulating French countryside, at last descending into Orly airport. In the past two days she had evolved into finally feeling like the High Priestess of the tarot, not just a pretender. Her two worlds had melded together, for the most part. Now it was time to save a member of the trionfi whom, even though she couldn't remember many of the details of their history together, she knew she loved deeply and had protected for many lives. It also meant saving the lives of countless unknown others upon whom Javier would seek his twisted revenge.

As the others departed the jet, Vesta waited for Liam who was posing for a photograph with the flight crew. After European-style air kisses on each cheek of each person Liam walked toward her with his jaunty gait.

"Well, that was a pleasant ride."

She looked at him without registering a response.

"What?" He lifted his hands up. "I thought you would be delighted that Donatella made her private jet available to us so quickly."

"It was a beautiful plane and very nice of her, but I would have been happy with an Air Force cargo plane, anything to get us back here."

"So here we are," Liam said with a smile.

"How can you act so happy?" Vesta scowled at him.

"I'm not happy, but I did enjoy the flight. And that gorgeous copilot and I are going to stay in touch."

"Whatever," Vesta said as she started walking. "I need to tell you something."

"Hey," Liam said grabbing her hand and gently pulling her to a stop. "I'm scared about what could happen to Peter, too. Remember, I'm the one who brought you into this whole thing."

"Well my InSight is working fine now. In fact, I saw him and Javier while we were in flight. Javier is not only threatening to kill Peter, he also plans to randomly have others killed who visit the cathedral if he doesn't get what he wants."

"Nasty piece of work, he is."

"And I heard him confess to killing his first wife."

Liam's eyes widened. "Do Grace and Luc know?"

"I doubt it, but I'm going to tell them. We're meeting at the taxi stand. Let's go."

On the sidewalk outside the airport Vesta said goodbye to Angeles.

"It was a great pleasure to meet you," the anthropologist said as she hugged her. "The secrets you share will always be safe with me, don't be concerned. But my work with the tarot will continue to expand, reflecting how we can all recognize and use our abilities to grow."

Vesta wrinkled her forehead while she and Grace watched Angeles get into a taxi and leave. "What did she mean by that?"

"She created a modified interpretation of the Thoth tarot deck based on her many cultural studies and astrological learning. It is a deck that has become very popular," Grace said.

"Aleister Crowley," Liam said who was eavesdropping and leaned in toward them. "Very strange dude, spent a wild week with him in Nepal once."

Abby waved for another taxi. "I'm sorry but I have to get back to my apartment. I just checked voice mail on my mobile. My professor can meet with me today to go over some things. My thesis is due next week. Horrible timing, I know. But I'm sure Luc and Liam will help you. Good luck Vesta. I know you will rescue Peter. And I will check in on the progress." She gave Vesta and Grace an air kiss on both cheeks.

"Good luck to you all!" Abby called out as she tossed her backpack into the seat of the taxi and hopped in. It pulled away from the curb as a silver van pulled up. Liam, Luc, Grace, and Vesta climbed inside and headed for the rue de Montaigne.

"Don't worry," Luc called out from the back seat. "We're about to put your plan into overdrive."

Vesta pressed her lips together. She hoped Luc was right. It was after three o'clock already. Sunset was only a few hours away.

Chapter Thirteen

P aris traffic was its usual snarled self, but at last they arrived at Grace's apartment. Her elegant home on the fourth floor lay silent as they stepped off the elevator. As she followed Grace and Luc through the living room toward the library, Vesta grabbed Liam by the arm holding him back.

"This color scheme of black, white and red is more than chic decoration. It embodies the alchemical story of the Garcia family, doesn't it?"

Liam paused and looked around.

"Definitely. Grace being the white queen and Javier the Red King. And his Basque heritage represented by the lauburu in the painting." He nodded as he took a longer look. "Yeah, The Great Work was described as beginning with black," he said eyeing the black symbol of the Basque culture. "It is the base, or starting point. White represents transformation into purity, and red is the perfection."

He looked over at the majestic *Le Vaisseau du Grand Oeuvre* painted by Grace's grandfather of her grandmother hanging above the fireplace.

"And this old girl completes the alchemical scene, doesn't she?"

Vesta stared into the dark eyes of the beautiful, naked woman encased in the glass beaker. "What would she think of what's happening now?" she asked. "Would either grandparent go to the lengths that Javier is willing to go to obtain the secret formula?" She felt like she already knew the answer and shivered.

"What are you doing!" Vesta heard Luc scream with an alarmed voice in French from another room. She ran toward it.

Inside a small white-paneled area off the dark-paneled library, the exact one she saw with her InSight the night before, Alejandro was sitting at a desk. In his hands rested a notebook, a page ripped partially from its spine. Luc and Grace stood beside him.

"Give that to me!" Luc shouted again in French. "That doesn't belong to you. You are destroying her grandmother's diary!"

"What is she saying?" Liam asked, his voice excited.

"Speak in English please Luc," Grace said while taking the notebook calmly from Alejandro.

Luc scowled in Liam's direction. "I'm saying that he is tearing apart something that doesn't belong to him."

"Thank you. I've never taken the time to learn French." He looked at Vesta and shrugged. "I guess I should."

Luc's face softened. "I'm sorry Liam. It's just that my brother has destroyed Grace's personal history."

"It belongs to all of us!" Alejandro shouted. "She has hidden what my father needs to know."

Luc began taking stacks of notebooks, pages yellowed and

scrawled with dates from the early nineteen-hundreds on their covers, off the desk.

"Your father," Luc hissed. "My father is willing to kill for this information. Did you know that? Do you want that blood on your hands, too?"

"You mean that lunatic who lurks in the cathedral?" Alejandro said as he stood up.

Hot blood flushed Vesta's cheeks at the mention of Peter in such an insulting way.

"I'm trying to save his life by finding the formula here in the notes. I found the letter from the old monk, the one in Basque. I translated it for father. That's how he knew crazy Peter had been given the secret."

"What are you saying Allie?" Grace said in a quiet tone putting her hand on his shoulder. He jerked away from her, walked to the window and turned to face the group.

"I taught myself to read the Basque language from the books in father's library. One day I noticed a letter lying on the floor beside your bookshelves." His gaze focused on Grace. "It looked like it had fallen from some papers on the shelf. I was surprised to see that it was written in that language, so I picked it up and began to read it for practice."

"I know the letter you speak of. It was at the back of one of my grandmother's diaries. I found it only recently." Grace looked around the room. "Where is it?"

"I gave it to father." Alejandro lifted his chin. "He has it."

"What did it say, Allie?"

Alejandro looked toward the neat rows of books and papers stacked along the white bookshelves.

"It was from a monk in Bilbao to his brother who lived here in the city. The letter explained that a priest who had just arrived from Paris was present for the last rites of Nicolas Flamel and heard him confess to solving the mystery of transmutation. He said Flamel gave the secret to Peter of Chartres Cathedral to hide for all eternity because no one else should know it or have that kind of power. The priest said he wanted to unburden his soul of the knowledge."

Alejandro looked toward the group, his raised eyebrows atop a satisfied smile on his face. "It made my father very happy to hear this."

"And tonight, he is going to kill Peter for that secret," Luc said taking a step toward him.

"Not if he gets the secret," Alejandro began.

"Peter won't give it to him," Vesta said.

"But he will return as the same person in another life even if he does die," the young man said.

"Alejandro!" Grace's shout startled Vesta as her voice reverberated off the walls of the room.

"It's true. I read it in my family history of the trionfi."

"That does not matter," Grace said returning her voice to a normal volume. "No life can be dismissed with a casual attitude."

"You see, Alejandro." Liam spoke up. "If he dies somewhere other than in that very cathedral, there are consequences that will rattle everything on the planet."

Alejandro jerked his attention toward Liam who responded with nod. "It's true."

"What consequences?" Alejandro asked.

"There's no time to go into that now, but let's just say that locusts could be involved."

Vesta shook her head. "What?"

"Not now, lovey. I'll tell you later. First let's find out where that tower is."

Alejandro crossed his arms over his chest. "I know where father is taking Peter."

"Where?" Luc asked.

"I'm not allowed to say."

"You must Allie," Grace said.

"Father trusted me with the information. I won't betray him."

"This is a matter of life or death you little weasel," Luc said taking another step toward him.

"Don't you dare touch me. I will tell Father. He already despises you for how you're wasting your life, your noise that you call music and your girlfriend."

Luc froze where she stood looking at her brother for a long moment before she spoke in a soft voice. "I'm going to say this because you need to hear it. Alejandro, I know you're gay too. And that you hide it."

A bright pink color rose on Alejandro's pale cheeks, his ebony-colored eyes flashed at his sister.

"It's okay. It's normal. Our mother's brother was gay also. She was so proud of him. Do you remember? She was flying to London to see him when the accident happened."

A knot twisted up in Vesta's stomach. She cleared her throat. Liam glanced at her.

"I know you have always wanted to please Father, but you can't let him murder someone," Luc said.

"I, um," Vesta said. "I need to tell you all something important." She ran her fingers through her hair.

"I won't tell you where they are Luc," Alejandro interrupted.

"You must," Luc said.

"No one can make me. And don't you dare tell Father that terrible lie you just made up."

"Please don't try to hide who you really are."

"You are the one who should be hiding."

"Mother knew too and encouraged Father to understand."

"Don't speak of Mother or her death again. I'm leaving now," Alejandro said making a move toward the door.

"Stop!" Vesta shouted. "He had her killed!" She blurted out the words.

"Who? What are you saying Vesta?" Grace looked at her with wide eyes.

Vesta ran her fingers through her hair again. "I'm sorry. It's just that you must hear this. Your mother's plane crash was no accident. Your father caused it."

Silence deafened the room. Grace, Luc, and Alejandro stared at her.

Vesta looked down at the floor. "It's true. I heard Javier say it himself, during one of my InSights."

"You lie!" Alejandro shouted.

"No." She shook her head. "I would never lie about this."

"Then you are wrong," he said with less force.

"She's never wrong about those sorts of things," Liam spoke up. "When she has those visions, it's like a motion picture running. It's her gift from the Elders."

A tear ran down Grace's cheek. "He is a monster."

"And we must stop him," Luc said.

Alejandro stared at a space somewhere between Grace and Vesta. Luc stepped close and wrapped her arms around him. He began to cry as he put his head on her shoulder.

"Why would he do such a thing?" Luc asked.

Grace wiped the tear from her face. "Perhaps I know. We had been introduced shortly before your mother died. At a cocktail party here at my house. Your father was immediately interested in my family history when he saw the painting of my grandmother."

"Are you saying he set up her death and married you to discover the secret?" Liam asked.

"It would explain many things."

"The Tour Saint-Jacques," Alejandro stammered as he wiped his own tears away. "He plans to take Peter there."

"Of course," Vesta said. "That's at the intersection of rue de Rivoli and rue Nicolas Flamel."

"But that's a national landmark," Luc said. "And no one is allowed inside because of the serious cracks in its walls."

"That's what makes it a perfect spot for Javier," Vesta said. "At dusk, people leave the park. I'm sure he has a way to gain access. No doubt he wants the irony rammed home to Peter that it is the burial place of the man who gave him the secret."

"Oh, so sick and fitting in his mind," Liam added.

"We will call the authorities," Luc said hugging Alejandro.

"And I am coming with you," Grace said.

"No! It's too dangerous," Vesta said.

"I will talk to Javier," Grace said. "Make him understand that murder isn't the way to discover what he wants."

"Serious doubts that he will listen to you," Liam said.

"He is my husband. I owe him that much to try."

Vesta exhaled and looked at Liam. "I understand where she's coming from. We'll keep her safe." She gestured toward Luc and Alejandro. "Don't call the police until I tell you to. I'll call you. If they arrive too soon Javier will take Peter someplace else. We can't risk that."

"Please take good care of her," Luc said reaching for Grace's hand. "She is our mother now."

Vesta smiled feeling tears seeping into her eyes and throat. "I will, I promise."

Grace drew Luc and Alejandro toward her hugging them and placing a kiss on each cheek. She turned to Vesta and Liam. "We should go."

Vesta looked at her wristwatch. "It's almost five-thirty. Traffic will be horrible, but sunset isn't for another hour or so."

Liam led the way to the elevators. A black Mercedes Benz

sat curbside in front of the building. A small man in a black jacket and white shirt hopped out of the car rushing to open the rear door for them.

"What's this," Vesta asked.

Liam shrugged. "I called for a car when we arrived here. Those mini-vans aren't for me."

"It's a mode of transportation, that's all."

He wagged his finger at her. "You have your proclivity for well-thought-out attire no matter the occasion." He waved his hand toward the sleek automobile. "And I have mine for travel."

"Fine," Vesta said as she slid into the back seat. "I'm going to tap into my InSight to see if I can connect with Peter, see where they are."

"Let me tell this good man where we're going then you can take off on your magical mystery tour and we'll keep our mouths shut so you can concentrate."

Vesta shook her head and smiled. "There you go with those old rock lyrics again."

She leaned her head against the headrest and closed her eyes. Inhaling solid, deep breaths she felt her body relax and her mind expand stretching its fingers toward infinity. The purring engine of the car died away and swirling white mist billowed toward her.

Chapter Fourteen

Peter looked more like a skeleton than a man. His normally wiry frame now contorted with drooping skin from the hollows of his cheeks, black circles under his eyes and a purplish-green colored jaw. He stood hunched holding the left side of his rib cage with his hand.

"Do you choose to die, saint?" Javier leaned against the simple desk in the now familiar dark spare room.

"I don't care if I die."

"No, of course not, because you will simply be born again, find your way to the church once more, and live your tranquil life." Javier stood up, stepping close to Peter. "But what if that were not so any longer?"

Peter looked up at him with his blue eyes shrouded in their black cases. A satisfied grin slipped across Javier's face like a chasm opening to reveal the entrance to hell below.

"Ah, now I have your attention." He began picking at the light brown tangle of hair on Peter's head. "It occurs to me that even though I don't have all the memories return to me each life, as you do, I have my diaries." He raised his eyebrows. "And I will write meticulous notes about how I must capture you once again in the next life and take you away from your precious church and kill you once again if you do not reveal the secret to me."

One by one Javier singled out hairs on Peter's head, plucking them one by one. "I will do this," he plucked a hair. "Life after life." He plucked another hair and let it fall to the floor. Then moving away from Peter, he gestured with his arms.

"I can live my life as I choose, still in luxury and power, but I will at some point come for you, maybe early in your life, maybe later. You will never know." He stepped close to Peter again, his breath on his purple-green jaw. "But you will know that I will be coming for you. Nothing will stop me. And you will begin to die, life after life, away from your cathedral." The ugly smile returned. "Do you want that, saint?"

Peter stared at him but said nothing.

"Get him out of here!" Javier shouted to Remy who stood in the doorway by the staircase. "Throw him in the back of the vehicle where you put the rest of the garbage."

Remy grabbed Peter by the shoulder ripping the sleeve of the black turtleneck sweater caked with dried mud. Remy's hand closed around the long bone of his arm and sagging skin draping over it. Peter winced as he stumbled through the doorway as Remy dragged him out.

Vesta's eyes flew open, a chill flooding her senses as the InSight faded away. "Oh my God."

Grace turned from the front seat to face her. Liam leaned in. "What?"

She looked toward the driver, shaking her head. "It's bad. I'll tell you later." Through the car window outside she could see the splendid gold nymphs riding their winged horses on the Pont Alexandre III as they drove past.

"It's getting close to six," she said.

Grace frowned. "Paris traffic." She waved her hand toward

the scene of cars and motorcycles jammed on the *quai*. "It is less than three kilometers from our home, but it takes so long sometimes."

Vesta knew there was nothing she could do but remain patient. Her right hand knotted into a fist as she thought about Javier's plan. His threat had unnerved Peter. Dying this time some place other than Chartres cathedral might be tolerable for him, but not life after life. The promise of that would taint every future life.

She eyed the Musee d'Orsay across the Seine and thought about all the leisurely times she had spent there which felt so long ago. The Place du Concorde, the tuilleries and the magnificent Louvre crept by on her left as they drove, past the Pont des Art and Pont Neuf they inched along on the Quai de la Mégisserie. Some of the most stunning parts of the city that she usually loved to soak in were a nuisance to her at the moment. Slowly the spires of Saint Chapelle grew larger on her right in the dimming sky as their car at last turned left on the boulevard Sébastopol revealing the Square Saint Jacques and its tower a block away on the right. The rue de Rivoli was on the far side of the park and traffic was as thick and sticky as peanut butter on toast moving on the thoroughfare.

"I'm going to jump out," Vesta said unable to bear the wait any longer.

"Yes," Grace said. "I will too."

"I guess that means the same for me," Liam said to the driver. "Wait for my call somewhere it's not so busy—Belgium, maybe."

The trio got out of the car and walked toward the Gothic stone tower with its narrow arched stained-glass windows halfway up its side. Tall metal posts with wire fencing in between surrounded the park. It was empty of people but Parisians heading home or to a café for a drink filled the sidewalks. Vesta scanned each face she passed searching for Peter or Javier.

"There is the entrance to the tower," Grace pointed. "But it is closed with a sign that says no admittance."

"I'm sure signs like that have never stopped Javier," Liam said pulling a cigarette from his shirt pocket.

"As I said, places like this are perfect for him." Vesta walked up to the gate and rattled it to see if it was unlocked. "Where's Sandor when I need him? He's good at getting into these things."

"You sent him on a wild goose chase to the catacombs two days ago, remember?" Liam slid his bright yellow Bic lighter out of his pocket and lit his cigarette.

Vesta glanced back at him. "How do you know that?" Her attention quickly shifted beyond him to a hulking figure pushing someone in a wheelchair on the sidewalk on the far side of the park. They were silhouetted by the diminishing light and appeared for only a few seconds in the clearing between the trees, but she recognized the heavy gait and large head. Drooping inside the wheelchair was a thin figure hunched over, more of shrouded mass than a man, and Vesta knew who it was.

"There they are!"

Liam and Grace turned from the gate to look where Vesta pointed. "See! Over there. They just turned the corner."

"Where?" Grace asked.

"Do you see the wheelchair and the man pushing it? On the other side of the park from us. They're just about to disappear behind the tower."

Vesta turned to Grace and Liam. "That means they still have to walk around the park to get to this gate."

"But that man looks too big to be Javier," Grace said.

"It's not Javier," Vesta said excitedly. "That is Remy, his hired thug and assassin. I saw him during my InSight."

"But where is Javier?" Grace asked.

"I don't know, somewhere close I'm sure." Vesta scanned the ground around them. She picked up a fist-sized rock that looked to be recently unearthed.

"What do you plan to do with that?" Liam asked as he let out a long puff of smoke.

"I'm going to hit Remy in the head with it so we can rescue Peter."

"Just like that?" Liam asked flicking his cigarette ash. "Quasimodo is going to walk up here and you're going to fell him with your little stone?"

"He isn't expecting to see us here. We're going to take him by surprise." Vesta looked toward a row of bushes standing nearby. "Let's hide in there and I'll jump out when they get to the gate." She looked back at Liam. "Simple but effective."

"I really would have thought you'd have a better plan."

"Shall we call the police?" Grace pulled her cell phone from the pocket of her trousers.

"Not yet. We need to wait until they are at the gate. I don't want them to escape." She turned to Liam. "Don't underestimate what my little stone and I can do. And besides, what would you do?"

"I'd call for backup," Liam said pulling in another long drag.

Vesta pushed her hair behind her ears. "I was planning to do this alone, anyway." She nodded toward the sidewalk. "You can leave now."

A silly smile spread across Liam's face. "I'm not going anywhere. I'm here to help you my pet. We have to rescue Peter."

"Okay, then shut up and get in the bushes."

"When Javier arrives, I will speak to him," Grace said. "I don't know that he will listen to me, but I can be a diversion while you deal with Remy."

Vesta looked at Grace clothed in white, shimmering in the gray light like a ghost haunting the ancient tower. She knew Grace would do whatever she could to help. Again, a warm feeling floated around her heart chakra. She smiled. "Thank you, my friend."

The trio walked behind the row of bushes which stood chest high next to the fence. Vesta, Liam, and Grace lined up and waited. Vesta focused on the corner of the park about thirty yards away where Remy and Peter should be turning the corner in a minute or two.

The tip of the cigarette glowed red as Liam pulled a long, hard drag then spoke. "So, what do you want me to do in this caper?"

Vesta kept her eyes on the corner. "Whatever is necessary. Don't you have some superpowers or something you can use?"

"I'm not bloody Superman."

"Just don't get in the way then. Where are they? They should have turned the corner by now." Vesta glanced at Liam quickly before returning her attention to the corner. "Did you come up on the short end of the gifts from the Elders? I haven't ever asked you what you can do."

"Hide and watch," Liam said. "Oh! Wait. That's what you're doing already." Liam blew out a final trail of smoke as he dropped the cigarette on the sidewalk and ground it out. Vesta felt a swoosh of air beside her and flicked her head toward it just in time to see Liam's feet rise past her eye level.

"He's flying!" Grace exclaimed.

Liam soared straight up over the fence disappearing toward the tower. Vesta stared at the empty space where he had been a moment earlier, then nodded to herself. That was a good gift, one she would like to have too.

"Where did he go?" Grace asked.

"I'm not sure. Maybe to the top of the tower." She returned

her attention to the sidewalk. Still no Remy pushing Peter. Irritation climbed up Vesta's spine. Where were they? Where was Javier?

As if in answer to the questions in her mind, Liam spoke through the fence. "There's a wheelchair on the other side of the tower."

"What?" Vesta said.

"It looks like they came in through the far side of the park," he said.

"Where's Peter then?"

"Inside the tower, I presume."

Red hot anger flashed through every cell in Vesta's body. Why didn't she consider that possibility? Here she stood hiding in some stupid bushes waiting for them while they strolled in from another direction. How could she have missed such an obvious alternative?

"Grace, let's get out of here." Vesta picked her way from behind the hedge and walked to the gate. Grace followed close to her.

"Okay, open the gate Liam," Vesta said.

Liam walked to face her. "I'm not a bloody locksmith like your boyfriend."

Vesta frowned for several reasons. "Then how are we going to get in? And he's not my boyfriend. Can you come get us and fly us over too?"

"Doesn't work that way. I'm spent for a while. It takes a lot of energy to do just that hop. But it appears the lock on the other side of the park has been picked. You should be able to get in there."

"Come on!" Vesta called to Grace as she began running for the corner. The two women turned left at the edge of the park and ran to the next corner and turned left again. A few yards down they found another gate with Liam standing beside it holding it open.

"Now what?" He said.

Vesta entered the park and saw a wheelchair sitting empty next to the steps of the tower. "They've gone up the tower." She began running toward it. When she reached the steps, she looked up to the cotton ball clouds in the sky turning a golden-orange.

"The sun is setting," Grace said.

"Let's go!" Vesta yelled as she ran up the stairs to the main platform, Grace and Liam on her heels. She paused there looking for an entrance to the stairs.

"Who is that fellow?" Liam asked standing next to her.

"Who?"

"That large stone dude there glaring down on us." Liam motioned up at an enormous statue on a pedestal in the middle of the landing. "It looks like he's making notes about us with that pen and scroll in his hand."

"Oh," Grace said. "That is Blaise Pascal. He is commemorated because of his studies on the atmosphere that were probably done here."

"How do you know such random information? I'm impressed," Liam said.

"My class came here once when I was a girl. I remember thinking it was odd to have a statue of a scientist here in the tower of the saint of butchers."

"The saint of butchers?"

"Yes, when it was built in the sixteenth century, it was part of the church of Saint-Jacques-de-la-Boucherie. All but the tower was torn down during the revolution."

"Enough chatter," Vesta said. "They had to have gone up this way." She walked to the spiral stairway tucked into a wall to begin climbing. Grace followed with Liam.

"I wonder how many steps there are up to the top of this old pile of stones," he said.

"Three hundred," Grace replied.

"That was a rhetorical question, but thanks for the information. I'm not sure if knowing that will make it easier or harder."

They began the trek up the ancient, narrow, dark stairs. Vesta set a brisk pace with Grace close behind and Liam lagging a few steps further back. A few minutes later they reached the first floor of the tower. Covered in dust with pigeons roosting in the corners for the night, Vesta scanned the room, but no sign of Peter existed.

"They're not here, let's keep going."

"Oh no, of course they would have to be at the top," Liam said as he followed the women further up the stairs. He began to count. "Just going to check your accuracy Grace," he puffed as they ascended.

At step seventy they arrived at another floor and walked into a vast space. Vesta looked up. In the orange glow of the early evening she could see the ceiling of the tower which extended far to the top. Narrow stained-glass windows on all sides of the tower at that level boasted golden medallions in the center with the letter F in a flourished style set ablaze in the setting sun.

"Is that a frilly F for Flamel?" Liam panted.

"Maybe," Vesta said.

"Where is the old boy buried?"

"He was buried under the floor of the tower," Grace said. "But no longer. The tower was excavated and raised to a new height in the eighteen-hundreds when the rue de Rivoli was created."

"So, only liters of dust and a pantheon of pigeons here now?"

"He took him to the top," Vesta declared as she surveyed the room then headed back to stairs.

"Yes, that seems to be the case," Grace said following Vesta. Liam fell in behind them and their trek continued.

"I've lost count on the stairs Grace," Liam said as he walked behind her and Vesta. "So, tell me something else about this moldy place to keep my mind occupied."

"Well," Grace began. "It captured the imagination of many writers. Alexandre Dumas was inspired to write a play called La Tour Saint-Jacques-de-la-Boucherie in the mid eighteen-hundreds."

"You're kidding," Vesta paused for a second.

"No, it is fact," Grace said.

Vesta began climbing faster. "Bastard. Thinks he's so clever."

"What are you mumbling about?" Liam asked not increasing his pace and lagging behind even more.

"During my InSight I found out that after Javier kidnapped Peter he took him to Château de Monte-Cristo, the house Alexandre Dumas built. He kept him in a little room and had that thug beat him."

"He is truly sick in the mind," Grace said. "And to spend the time to create such a wicked plan."

"He probably thought it was amusing to tie it all together," Liam said between gasps of breath. "The fact Flamel gave Peter the secret and was buried here for a while, and that it was connected to a Dumas play which was connected to his house."

"Yeah, we got it," Vesta said setting a pace that was almost a run.

"Fine! I'm just trying to break up the monotony," Liam called out as he heaved air into his lungs. "How can you run up these bloody stairs?"

"Remember, I grew up on the side of a mountain," she said as she sprinted.

Minutes passed that felt like hours to Vesta. She knew the sun had probably set and despite Javier's threats Peter would never share the secret with him. She increased her pace until her lungs were crying out desperately for more oxygen. Push harder, she demanded. The ceiling was close now, and beyond that, the roof. Keep pushing. She had saved Peter centuries earlier by designing Chartres Cathedral for him. A place he could feel safe and comfortable to live out his lives in peace where his personal struggles for meaning could be contemplated by walking the labyrinth. Even though she couldn't remember the details, she could feel within her heart, perhaps her soul, that she had saved him.

Her feet landed on the top floor of the tower. The stairs leading to the roof were narrow and laden with dust but she could see even in the dim light that fresh footprints lay on them. Her pulse quickened as she ran up the stairs and burst through the little door onto the roof. She gasped and froze in place as her eyes took in the scene.

Chapter Fifteen

J avier stood on the roof in a perfectly tailored black suit with a small red rose in his lapel. Next to him was Remy, dressed in gray work pants and a long-sleeved black t-shirt. Suspended from Remy's outstretched arm was a gangly mass of black arms and legs with a head and torso drooping almost lifelessly.

"Peter!" Vesta screamed. Javier jerked his head toward her voice.

"My Vesta, you're here!" Peter's voice was just above a whisper.

"So, our saint was able to communicate his location to our High Priestess." He waved his hand toward Remy and Peter. "No matter. If you come closer, my friend here will toss him to the ground like a bag of garbage."

"No! Wait!" Vesta yelled, her vocal cords scraping against her throat like she had been lost in the desert for a week. Behind her she heard the stamping of feet as Grace rushed up beside her.

"Oh, *mon Dieu!* Javier! What are you doing?" Grace's voice peeled through the air like a bell.

Javier glared at her. "I knew you betrayed me. When you disappeared, I knew it was to help this fool."

"You've got that wrong," Liam called out between panting breaths as he cleared the stairs and stepped onto the roof. "I'm the Fool. And I'm here to help her."

"What an amusing group." The demonic smile Vesta viewed during her InSight slid back into place across his face. "The addled High Priestess who cursed herself, a bumbling Fool who sings silly songs, and my despicable wife."

He turned back toward Remy and Peter. "Your saint will either tell me what I want to know, or he will die."

"Javier," Grace said. "I know you despise me now, but I appeal to the man I married. The one who was kind and gentle." She took a step toward him. "This can't be what you truly want to do. His murder will be etched on your soul forever."

"The man you married never existed. It was all a pretense to gain unlimited access to your grandparents' laboratory journals." His smile dissolved. "I never loved you. You have no royal blood in my house of Pentacles." Javier sneered at Grace. "You were never anything more than an obstacle I had to maneuver around."

Grace stood still, her short dark hair floating around a beautiful face, her pale skin and white clothing creating the sense that the goddess Moon touched down on Earth that evening for a visit.

"You killed your first wife. I saw that with my InSight. Was she an obstacle too?" Vesta shouted.

"She was not only an obstacle but a liar and adulterer. But that was many years ago, the plane crashed into the sea. You would never be able to prove anything."

"We'll see about that." Vesta stepped beside Grace. "Now turn Peter loose or I will call the police." She fished her cell phone out of her little Hermes bag slung across her chest.

"You will say I pushed him. I will say you did. Remy will say you did." Javier waved his hands in the air. "The police will not know who to believe. And I have known the police captain for quite a long time. I think he might believe me. Then where would that leave you?"

"You mean you would buy off the captain," Liam said taking two steps forward to stand next to Vesta and Grace.

"You would do this for money, Javier?" Grace asked.

"Having pure gold made with my own hands will make me legendary," He rubbed his hands together. "But the secret that Flamel possessed will give me something even better."

Javier paused, looking out from the tower. Vesta followed his gaze noticing her surroundings for the first time. The sky had turned a blood red as the rays of the sun dipped below the romantic peaks of the Ile-St-Louis. She had a three-hundred-sixty-degree view of Paris being bathed in the last glow of the sun. Despite the urgent matter in front of her, Vesta took in a silent gasp at the scene. From this vantage point she could see the Eiffel Tower in one direction, Sacré-Coeur far in the distance in another, and the brutalist architecture of the Pompidou Center close by in the opposite direction.

Peering out from the roof in one corner high above them was a statue of Saint Jacques holding a huge meat cleaver in his hand honoring the butchers who contributed the largest amount of money to build the church four hundred years earlier. In another corner knelt an angel keeping watch over the city and in the far corner where Javier, Remy, and Peter stood a griffin statue sat triumphally on its perch just behind them.

"What will the secret give you that's even better than money, Javier?" Grace asked.

Vesta heard Grace's question and quickly refocused her attention. "Turn Peter loose Javier and you can leave," she said.

A cackle seeped out of his mouth that was so sharp that it

could have widened the cracks in the crumbling stone of the tower.

"You don't understand, I'm going to become immortal, even better than you, your Highness, when I obtain the formula."

"You'll turn into a bloody monster," Liam said.

"That is a matter of opinion," Javier said.

"Most of the others became ungodly scourges upon the Earth." Peter spoke up.

"And we had a devil of a time either finally killing them or corralling them," Liam added.

Vesta frowned realizing she needed to know more about what Liam mentioned, but now wasn't the time to ask.

"Turn him loose now," she said again.

Javier turned to Peter. "Saint, this is your last chance before you plunge to your death. This time away from your church. Where is Flamel's secret?"

"You'll never have it." Peter's voice was stronger.

"Fine," Javier waved his hand. "Remy."

The hulking man with the stubble on his head and face who still held Peter by the arm, swung the frail man toward the edge of the tower.

"No!" Vesta and Grace screamed together.

In the rapidly thickening night, Vesta felt a whoosh of air beside her. The same whoosh as earlier. She saw Liam jettison off the stone roof of the tower flying toward Remy and Peter like a missile. He landed a punch with his fist squarely in Remy's throat. Pain howled from the large man as he turned loose of Peter and grabbed his throat. Liam landed on the parapet for only a second before he wrapped his arm around Remy's neck and jerked him over the side of the tower. Both men disappeared into the now black sea of night. Peter fell against the short wall of the tower then dropped to the floor in a heap.

"Oh my God!" Vesta screamed. She and Grace ran to the

parapet where Liam and Remy fell. Javier strode to Peter grabbing him by the arm and hoisting him up onto the ledge. Below, a streetlight on the corner shone enough light that she could see Remy sprawled in an unnatural position on the ground, his body clearly lifeless. Beside him stood Liam barely visible in his solid black outfit, brushing himself off.

"Liam! You're okay?" she yelled down to him.

"I'm good. My plan worked perfectly." He glanced down at his jeans. "Well, almost. I ripped my trousers as I flew into one of those thorny bushes." He pointed toward the fence where a hedge row stood. "I'll head back up. Can't fly for a bit though. Have to take those bloody stairs again. Take care of Peter alright?"

Vesta exhaled, feeling sweat run down her spine. "Yes! I'll make sure Peter is okay." She turned back toward the roof to see Javier heaving Peter onto the top of the parapet.

"Get away from him," her voice roared with a depth that surprised even her. The guttural sound must have caught Javier off guard too because he stopped pushing Peter and stared at her for a moment, his eyes opening wide, devouring her image. It was long enough for her to rush forward to the two of them, pushing Javier away from Peter. She could feel brittle bone through the cotton cloth of his turtleneck sweater as she grabbed him, his torso so lightweight that both of them toppled to the floor of the roof in a sprawl.

"Your necklace," Javier stammered.

Vesta looked up at him, not knowing what to say. She jumped to her feet to stand in front of Peter. Javier reached inside his jacket pocket and pulled out a stubby knife. He took two steps and grabbed Grace by the waist who was looking toward Vesta. He pulled her in front of him, placing the knife at her throat. The laugh that could crack ancient stone walls screeched from his lips.

"He gave you the secret." His dark eyes flashed so that even in the dim nighttime light she could see the anger. "Give it to me or she dies just like that imbecile Remy."

"What are you saying about my necklace?" Vesta shook her head completely confused by his words.

"Vesta," Peter mumbled. "Let me see your necklace."

She backed up beside Peter never taking her eyes off of Javier and bent down.

"Where did this come from?" Peter asked lifting his hand toward her.

"Liam gave it to me."

A weak smile moved across Peter's face. "Always the clever man."

"What? What do you mean?" Vesta glanced at his face for an answer.

Peter winced, adjusting his hunched position. "These are the stones Nicolas gave me and asked me to protect. I sent them to Liam when I knew the Red King was after them." He pointed a trembling finger toward Javier.

Vesta felt a flush of clarity wash over her as she fingered the stones. "Did you get these from the crypt near the well? Under that mural of the hand reaching out between the moon and stars?"

Peter nodded feebly.

"The way to turn base material into gold is encrypted on there." He squinted at Javier. "And how to deliver immortality to a human body if you know how to read those symbols correctly."

Vesta's eyes glanced toward the necklace then slid up to look at Javier and Grace.

"Yes, that's right." Javier sneered. "And I know how to read the formula." He pressed the knife closer to Grace's throat. "I found it in the laboratory diary of her grandfather. He had drawings of those stones with the markings, and the order to put them in. He became immortal from using them."

"My grandfather is dead and buried here in Paris," Grace said.

Javier looked at Grace cackling with his mouth close to her ear. "He led everyone to believe that." His eyes cut toward Vesta. "Now give me that necklace or Grace will make a less than graceful exit."

"Wait." Vesta stood up. "I'll give you the necklace."

"No, Vesta!" Grace shouted. "I am not afraid to die."

Adrenaline spiked through Vesta's body from her head to her toes. "I won't let you die!"

"Vesta," Grace said. "If Javier uses this secret, he will bring more destruction and death."

"I can't let you die," Vesta said as her hands began to sweat.

"He will become a plague," Peter said quietly. "Unstoppable. I have seen it. If he gets the stones."

"I will stop him. I promise," she said to Peter.

She lifted the necklace from around her neck and let it drop into her hand. She looked at the oddly shaped colored stones marked with what she had thought were careless scratches, lines and circles. She rubbed the silver crescent moon with her thumb and thought of the night a week ago, but that seemed like a lifetime, when Liam had given it to her at dinner at Le Bernardin's. Sandor was there making a joke about the gift box not holding a bowling ball. Javier and his children sat at another table with Amara and Jared. It was the first time she had laid eyes him, and now he was threatening to kill two people she loved. And she held the key to their safety.

"Here." She reached her hand out, the necklace dangling from it. "It's yours."

"No, Vesta," Grace screamed.

"Bring it to me," Javier said, the pupils of his eyes narrowing.

Vesta stepped toward them, Javier holding the knife against Grace's throat with his right hand, his left outstretched.

"That's far enough," he said as she stood two arm's lengths away.

She placed the necklace in his hand. His fingers closed tightly around the stones and she could hear him exhale a satisfied breath.

"He will kill me anyway," Grace said in a calm voice.

Javier flicked his head toward Grace as though he had momentarily forgotten about her. The viper's smile crept into view as he glanced toward Vesta. "She's right, you know."

With a swift jerk he hauled Grace on top of the parapet giving her a hard push that sent her slipping over the side of the tower.

"Grace!" Vesta screamed loud enough for the angels in heaven to hear. "You evil bastard!"

She rushed at him with all her force shoving him against the wall. The knife and the necklace fell from his hands. They grappled for the knife before Javier retrieved it and stabbed Vesta in the right shoulder. More than hurting from the sharp piece of metal that pierced her flesh and muscle, Vesta hurt from the thought of her friend laying on the ground below.

Vesta let out a howl, she tried to get up to grab Javier who had jumped to his feet and grabbed Peter once again.

"Your turn," he said easily dragging Peter toward the parapet.

"But you have the necklace. You have what you want," Vesta yelled, her throat brittle. She leaned on the left side of her body to stand up. The stab wound wasn't deep, but it stung.

"He serves no purpose to me and has been more trouble than he could ever be worth."

Javier dragged Peter's body which offered no resistance

except for dirty black loafers that scuffled against the dusty stone toward the parapet. Out of the corner of her eye, Vesta saw something she couldn't quite explain with her thoughts or words. Space seemed to shift in front of her like a transparent wave that moved across her vision. It was three-dimensional, distorting the lights of the nearby buildings as it moved from the doorway across the roof.

The next moment she saw Javier bolt forward over the edge of the parapet leaving Peter lying face down on the ledge. Vesta blinked hard not understanding what she just witnessed. As she stared a wiggly image began to form, a solid figure taking the shape of a man.

"Sandor?" she stammered.

Dark hair slicked back in his stylish way, wearing a deep purple polo shirt and navy trousers, he stood fully formed next to Peter.

"Another case of impeccable timing," Sandor said as he looked over the edge of the tower. "What the hell?" he called out. "Aren't you the lucky bastard?"

"Am I hallucinating?" Vesta said more to herself than anyone else as she scrambled to her feet and raced to Peter. His body lay still with open eyes. "Peter!"

"I am alive, regardless of how I must look," he said. "Is it over?"

"Yes," Vesta said.

"Not quite." Sandor was pointing on the other side of the parapet wall. Vesta walked over to where he stood.

"Oh no!"

When Sandor pushed Javier away from Peter, he had fallen over the low wall landing on one of the ornamental stone gargoyles that also served as a rain spout. His body lay on top of it with one leg swinging in the air.

"Help me," he shouted.

"Forget it man," Sandor said straightening up and walking toward Peter.

Vesta looked at Sandor. "We can't just leave him there."

"I can." Sandor bent over to help Peter sit up. "Call the cops with the cell phone you could have used to call me."

"Your Highness, please help me," Javier called out.

Vesta peered over the edge of the tower again. Far below him to the left, in the yellowish glow from the streetlight, she could see the bodies of Remy and Grace splayed out like tiny plastic action figures on the ground. Nausea bubbled up inside her, then a seething anger. Javier should suffer the same fate. He pushed his wife to her death. He killed Grace, her friend, someone who she knew could be trusted, someone who cared about her, someone she loved in return.

A tear rolled down her cheek. She had never felt friendship like that before with another woman. Gentle yet strong, honest and fearless, she wasn't trying to suck up to her for a job in Sybarite or sabotage her to get her own job as women had tried to do in the past. Grace was a true friend, and Javier killed her.

"Help me, please," the king of Pentacles pleaded, clutching the neck of the medieval monster so that it looked like he was riding it bareback. "This is so old, I'm afraid it will break."

He stretched his left arm up toward her, easily within her reach. Vesta stared at his hand grasping for hers. The same hand that held Grace and Peter minutes earlier with the intention of murdering them. He deserved to die, yet an infuriating voice inside her head pricked at her saying she was not the one to decide who dies. She swatted at it with other thoughts, but it persisted. Her cheeks flushed pink with the angry knowledge that she would help him.

"Look!" he said as his eyes shifted to something just below her. "It's the necklace. It's yours."

Following his gaze, Vesta saw her necklace dangling from a

small hunk of ancient ornamentation protruding from the parapet. She picked it up from the knob of weathered stone, unzipped her purse and placed it inside.

"I'm calling the police first," she announced to not only him but the niggling voice in her head that argued for not rescuing him. Several feet away her phone lay on the stone floor, she walked over, picked it up and notified them of their location.

"Tell them to send an ambulance too," Sandor said, his arm around the Hanged Man of the tarot, holding him upright. "Peter's in pretty bad shape. Nothing I can fix."

Vesta's stomach twisted into a knot. Peter had to be okay. He must return to Chartres. She asked for an ambulance then disconnected the call.

"Your Highness!" The voice of Javier wavered in the stillness of the early night. "Please help me."

"Let the cops handle it," Sandor said catching her eye.

From a rational standpoint she knew he was right. Leave Javier alone and let the police deal with him. But something deep inside her, in the very structure of her DNA, overruled common sense and compelled her to help him. She turned her gaze back toward the voice, she paused, but only for a moment before walking toward it.

Looking over the edge once more, she asked. "Why should I help you?"

Javier struggled to sit up on the medieval steed below him. "Because I went temporarily mad," his words stammering and rapid. "I didn't know what I was doing. I hate myself for what happened to Grace."

"Don't!" Vesta shouted at him. "Don't speak her name." The hot pink blood rushed to her face again. "You aren't worthy to even say her name."

"Alright." He laughed nervously. "Alright. I understand."

He stretched his trembling hand out as far as he could. "Just please help me."

Beneath Javier's body, she heard the sound of a pop like a rock busting on a cement sidewalk.

"It's cracking!" Javier yelled.

Vesta knew he was right. The sculpture that looked like a mashup of a dog and dragon had bent midway along its body, the weight of Javier too much for its eight-hundred-year-old frame. If nothing else, Vesta reasoned to herself, I'm going to save this historical landmark, but she knew as much as she was unwilling to admit it that she was saving Javier.

Bracing herself against the short wall of the parapet she leaned over. "Grab my hand," she said. "Try to grab my wrist too, and I'll grab yours."

As she reached out her right hand, she felt a dull ache in her right shoulder where Javier had stabbed her. She looked down at the blood drying on her sweater. The knife hadn't torn through anything life threatening but the pain was sharp. Javier noticed her looking at the blood.

"Oh, your Highness, I'm so sorry. I was momentarily out of my mind. Please forgive me and help me."

Another cracking sound came from underneath Javier as they both saw the head of the gargoyle detach falling to the into the abyss of the night. Javier screamed and lifted his body. Vesta grabbed his sweat-soaked hand and wrist, anchored her knee against the wall and pulled as hard as she could. Hot pain shot through her shoulder. She threw her left hand onto Javier's forearm jerking him toward her with all the strength she had. He scrambled up and off the ancient stone rain spout, throwing himself onto the ledge of the parapet. As he grabbed it with both hands Vesta turned loose of him and clutched her shoulder which had begun to bleed again.

"Thank you. Thank you so much," Javier said as he hauled himself onto the stone floor.

Sandor stood up. "I would have left you there."

"Yes, I know," Javier said as he appeared to brush dust off his jacket but instead reached for an inside pocket and pulled out a knife casing. He flicked it open exposing a knife, shorter and wider than the other one. He grabbed Vesta by her sweater and jerked her next to him. She could feel the warm blade next to her throat. Stepping further back from Sandor, Javier pulled Vesta with him so that they stood against the parapet in the corner of the tower.

"I know you would have let me die, but the priestess," his hot breath coming out in spurts close to her ear. "She could not. Valentina was right when she told me how to block your precious InSight and that you were always a sympathetic fool. Especially for believing someone like me. And don't try that disappearing act again," he said as he looked toward Sandor pressing the knife tighter against her throat. "This time I will not turn her loose."

"If you cut her again, I will tear you apart with my bare hands." Sandor spoke in a calm voice staring with unblinking eyes at Javier. "And you have no idea what you will unleash if you try to conjure with those stones."

"It's my destiny to be immortal. I am the Red King whose ruby blood is meant to rule over the masses!" Javier shouted. "I can be a benevolent monarch when my subjects allow it. When they bend the knee to me in recognition of my Divine authority."

"You're completely mad," Vesta said.

Javier looked toward the door. "Now, the High Priestess and I are going to walk down the stairs. If you follow, I will cut her throat."

Vesta closed her eyes. She did feel like a fool for saving

Javier's life even though she knew she had no other choice. The sharp blade against her skin lusted for blood, she could feel it, and these could be her last thoughts in this life. But the same inner voice that demanded she pull Javier to safety also assured her there was a way to escape from him.

Behind her eyelids an image came into view of Javier standing as he was at that moment, the knife poised against her throat. Her attention was drawn to a glowing red spot she saw on his right hip. Grace had mentioned it had been injured years earlier in a motorcycle accident. It was the weakest spot on his body, and he felt pain there still, her inner knowing said to her.

Gathering every molecule of strength she could muster in her body, she opened her eyes, spotted his right hip, aimed her right elbow, and sent a powerful blow to the area landing exactly on target. Javier let out a sharp cry and crumpled to his right, turning loose of Vesta and grabbing his hip. As he did, he lost his balance and fell over the edge of the tower, this time with no Gothic monster to catch him. Vesta leaned over the parapet and watched him fall into the pit of darkness, a dull thud announced his arrival on the ground. In her mind she saw the horror of three bodies strewn carelessly like discarded toys next to the tower. She squeezed her eyes shut.

"It's okay." Sandor's embrace felt strong and sure as he grabbed her. "It's all over, baby."

They could hear sirens in the distance getting closer.

Chapter Sixteen

A flood of flashing lights and voices filled the air around the tower of Saint-Jacques. Police hiked up the three hundred stairs and called for a stretcher when they saw Peter. Sandor explained the situation in simple terms that he, Peter, and Vesta agreed would be their story. Javier believed his wife was having an affair with Peter and hired Remy to kill them both in a set-up on top of the roof. He and Vesta were contacted by Peter and came to help. Javier pushed Grace off the tower and a struggle ensued that ended up with both Remy and Javier falling to their deaths. Crimes of passion, something the French well understood. Of course, they would need statements from all the surviving parties, but it looked to be a closed case.

Peter was transported to Hospital Hotel-Dieu nearby in the fourth arrondissement. Vesta kissed him on his pale forehead before they strapped him onto the stretcher and carried him down the winding staircase. Promising to follow the paramedic's advice to have her own wound checked out, she and Sandor descended the stairs to find Liam standing on the bottom landing beside the statute of Blaise Pascal smoking a cigarette.

He nodded up toward the towering stone man who stared back down on them in return.

"We've become good mates while I waited for you two."

"I thought you were coming back to help," Vesta said.

"I saw Sandor here as he began running up those ghastly stairs. I'm the one who called him to tell him where we were going and what was happening." He took a long drag. "And I took care of that neanderthal Javier hired," he said blowing out the smoke. "I knew the two of you had the rest of it handled."

"Javier pushed Grace off the tower."

"I heard her hit the ground. Sorry, love. I could tell you grew close to her."

Tears welled up in Vesta's eyes. She brushed them away and shoved her hair behind her ears. "Yes, she was my friend."

The hardest part, she realized, was that Grace was just human. She died and wouldn't come back in the next life as Grace. In her next incarnation she would be someone, or maybe something else. Entirely unaware of the love and beauty she brought to the world and the sacrifice she made.

Sandor put his arm around Vesta and drew her to him, being careful not to squeeze too hard. "Did you know he also stabbed Vesta?"

Liam knitted his eyebrows and scanned her until he noticed the dried blood on the shoulder of her sweater. She saw a flash of pink in his cheeks, but he recovered immediately.

"You're a tough old bird," he said, his zig-zag grin creasing his face. "You don't look any worse for the wear."

"I'm going to the hospital now to wait on word about Peter."

"He did look a bit rough as they carried him past me." Liam ground out his cigarette on the dusty stone floor then picked it up and placed the butt in his pocket. "I'll check in on him later."

Vesta walked down the steps from the platform onto the grass. Two policemen hurried past her while two more at the gates were directing a crowd of onlookers to move back. She turned, looking behind her to see little pools of light searching the ground where three bodies lay, one being Grace. The horrible, gruesome scene played out in her mind like the loop of a movie clip. Each time she watched her friend shoved over the edge of the parapet her heart felt a pain. She let it replay over and over without trying to block it, thinking the pain would become less sharp as the replay wore on, but it didn't.

She and Sandor rode in silence in the back of a police car to the hospital. There, they each gave their official statements for the police record. She repeated Sandor's version of the story and knew Peter would too when he was strong enough to talk. As preposterous as it actually was, it would make the most sense to police. The truth, that the head of an ancient household sought the secret to turn lead into gold and make himself immortal kidnapped a living member of the tarot cards, was too fanciful to ever be believed. It was even difficult for her to believe as she lay it out in words. Then to explain that she, another member of the tarot, along with two more, came to his rescue using their superhuman gifts given by beings she still couldn't exactly describe, was bordering on lunacy to anyone who would listen. Sandor's story was the way to go.

A doctor examined her, and a nurse treated her stab wound which turned out to have inflicted only minor damage to the muscle. They wanted to put her arm in a sling, but she refused. Her injury was so minor compared to Peter who suffered a broken jaw, three broken ribs, a collapsed lung, and severe dehydration. Despite that, he begged to be released from the hospital and to be taken to Chartres. The priests at the cathedral had offered to tend to him in his room at the Hôtellerie Saint-Yves. Sandor arranged for his transport in an ambulance and hired a nurse to stay with him until his wounds had healed and he could walk again.

When Vesta picked up her cell phone to call for a car to drive her to Le Parvis, Sandor smiled at her.

"I had the things you left there and your bag at the Garcia home taken to the Hotel du Jeu de Paume." He pulled a fresh red rose from inside his trouser pocket and handed it to her. "I thought you might be more comfortable there."

A car waited for them as they left the hospital. Walking through the old passageway off the rue Saint-Louis en l'Île, past the half-timbers plastered into stucco walls, into the cozy chic interior courtyard, up the elevator to her favorite room with the large white marble bathtub, Vesta felt emotion swarm over her; relief but deep grief, gratitude but guilt, anger yet hope.

"I'm in the room next door," Sandor said gently as he handed her the key. "Get some rest and we'll talk tomorrow." He kissed her on the cheek and closed the door behind him.

It was past ten o'clock. Parisians would be wrapping up dinner and heading for a stroll along the *quais* or out to a club, maybe having an intimate drink with friends at a neighborhood bar. Vesta turned the faucets in the tub on full blast. She winced as she pulled her torn, dirty sweater set over her head. All she wanted was a hot bath, but it was guilt that washed over her as she slipped beneath the surface of the water.

Peter lay in the hospital at that moment in agony, she was sure, not so much from his injuries even though they were significant, but from the gaping wound of being away from his cathedral. It would be tomorrow before he would be transported to Chartres.

Her thoughts turned even more sad and dark as she thought that also at that moment Grace lay cold and still in a morgue somewhere in the bowels of Paris. Vesta began to cry and this time she let the tears flow like rain from a cloud-filled sky. Grace knew she was risking her life to fly to Italy, to the Paneveggio Forest to tell her about Javier's plan. She knew the danger when she insisted on coming with her to the tower of Saint-Jacques. Vesta heard her last words echo in her head. "I'm not afraid to die," she said.

Sinking her head below the water in the bathtub, Vesta wished the memory would wash away, cleansing her mind of that moment.

"No," she said out loud as she raised her head above the water. "I want to remember."

She felt the deep pain within her chest. It wasn't a physical pain, but a soul pain that began to transform into something... other. How could she describe it? It was like something sticky and dark cracking open to reveal another aspect of itself that was pure and full of—Vesta paused because she knew what the next word in her thought was—love. But her feeling deserved a better word than that. Something that transcended the word that people so casually threw out about each other or food or the color of a new pair of socks. This sensation, this understanding, required a new word. Grace would understand what she meant. Vesta smiled. She would keep her friend's memory alive and celebrate it through something new she would create.

Her next thought surprised her. She was starving. When was the last time she ate? It was in Italy, for sure, but she couldn't remember exactly when. A phone sat on a small table within arm's length of the bathtub. After she reached for it, she called Sandor's room. He sounded happy to hear her voice and her plans.

An hour later, clean and outfitted in the finest Chanel dress she brought with her, she and Sandor stepped out onto the rue Saint-Louis en l'Île and into a car for the short ride to Le Meurice on rue de Rivoli. She walked into the stunning dining room filled with marble and golden moldings, a wall of mirrors and a forest of chandeliers, white linen tablecloths and tuxedoed waiters. Liam sat in a corner banquette dressed in fresh black leather and smoking a French cigarette.

"You are my girl," he said standing up and embracing her. "Welcome to turning the corner."

Sandor spoke quietly to the maître d' who waved to a waiter standing nearby. Vesta slid into the banquette next to Liam and Sandor followed in beside her. The waiter arrived at the table with a bottle of 1979 Dom Pérignon, filled the flutes in front of them then left.

Picking up his glass, Sandor eyed Vesta for moment before he spoke. "You've come a long way, in a short time. Here's looking at you, kid."

Vesta smiled. "Thanks. At least you didn't use an old lyric from a rock song."

"Hey!" Liam said. "Some of the best poetry of this age has come from rock lyrics." He tipped his glass to his lips.

Vesta looked at her glass for a moment and nodded before she took a sip. The pale golden liquid slipped down her throat like children's laughter on a spring morning. She leaned back in the seat and gazed around the room.

"Don't feel guilty," Liam said.

She looked at him wondering if he was reading her thoughts.

"I'm not reading your thoughts."

Vesta blinked. "Yes, you are."

"No, I'm really not. I just know what a look like that at a time like this means." He took another sip from his glass. "Because I once had the same thoughts."

"I've seen some of that," she said. "Despite your official description of the Fool being light-hearted even during times of stress and trauma."

Liam raised his eyebrows.

"Yes, I've done my research on all the members of the tarot

according to what's printed in books." She sipped her champagne. "When you went against my wishes—I won't call it betrayal anymore—and called Sandor and the others to the Villa Spada. I knew you were crushed by my anger, my hurt."

Liam looked down at the table.

"And also, when you told us that Peter was missing, fearing he had been kidnapped, I saw your fear then too."

"I'm not supposed to feel that way." He looked up at her, brushing a clump of brown hair away from his left eye. "It makes me less capable at the job I'm here to do."

Vesta put her hand on his. "It makes you more human." She looked at Sandor. "And that makes us all better."

Pointing at her necklace, Liam said. "I had that made for you because I knew you would keep it safe. I knew I couldn't find Peter without your help."

"Why didn't you tell me what it was?"

"Too much of a burden."

Vesta nodded. "I guess it would have been."

"Tonight," Sandor began. "You have come into your own as the High Priestess. You understand not only what your job is and how to do it well, but you have shifted into that place that we"—he pointed toward Liam with his glass—"understand and accept." Sandor set his champagne down and pulled a white rose from his jacket pocket and placed it on the table.

Vesta felt tears threaten again.

"We move through life after life meeting many, many people. Most mean little or nothing to us, but some"—he placed his hand on the rose—"mean a lot to us."

"What will Luc and Alejandro do with her grandparents' alchemy diaries and lab journals?" she asked trying to put her thoughts on something concrete.

"I'm going to suggest they donate them to the Warburg Institute," Liam said. "The place is filled with crazy stuff. It'll fit right in. Minus the secret formula of course." He nodded at her necklace. "That's for you to hold on to."

Vesta touched one of the stones feeling the deep grooves cut into it. "I have become rather fond of this. And it will always remind me of Grace." She smiled.

Sandor picked up his glass. "Our hearts could have felt like leaden boxes, for me and Liam, that we endlessly dragged around with us life after life, but like you tonight, we learned to move through the process of grief over these lifetimes and came to realize that being grateful and celebrating the lives of those we loved, understanding that we must turn loose of any possession we feel is the best way to honor our duties as members of the trionfi and them as the friends we made along the way."

Vesta wiped away another persistent tear that welled up in the corner of her eye.

"Sandor, that's so beautifully said. I've never heard you be so eloquent."

"Hah!" Liam laughed as he raised his glass. "He's a master at it. You just don't recall those days when we all hung out at the Globe."

Vesta shot a glance at Sandor. "What?"

Sandor smiled at her. "Doll, that's a story for another day."

THE END

Read the next book in the series, The Seven Pentacles Prophecy.

Vesta must unravel an ancient prophecy to stop a murderous immortal—or risk the fate of the world and the lives of those she holds most dear.

When oracles foretell of a devastating upheaval, she finds herself thrust into her most dangerous challenge yet. A homicidal immortal has surfaced, intent on bringing the prophecy to fruition, and his actions threaten to upend everything Vesta and the trionfi have worked to protect.

Join Victoria's newsletter (victoriabelue.com) to receive free bonus chapters and novellas, plus the latest news about new releases, including her upcoming series, The Fairforest Witches debuting in 2025.